MW00451876

DON'T TELL

The Secrets of Pinehurst Seminary

Julie A. Kennedy

Don't Tell: The Secrets of Pinehurst Seminary
Copyright 2019 by Julie A. Kennedy

All rights reserved under International and Pan-American Copyright Conventions. No part of this book may be reproduced in any form or by any means, electronic or mechanical, including photocopying, recording, or by any information storage and retrieval system, without permission in writing from the publisher, except by a reviewer who may quote brief passages in a review.

ISBN: 978-1-949810-05-9

The Florida Historical Society Press
435 Brevard Avenue
Cocoa, FL 32922
http://myfloridahistory.org/fhspress

PRESS

Dedication

In loving memory to my grandfather, Herman Henry Conrader. Although I never knew you in life, I got to know you through stories Mom told me. She told me the story about your time at Pinehurst when I was a child. More than one hundred-ten years have passed since you were at the school, and the story has faded into oblivion. I wrote this book to revisit the experiences and memories of the children at Pinehurst and to share it with others.

Acknowledgments

Writing and publishing a book is not a one-person venture; it takes teamwork. I feel blessed with the team I worked with in order to bring this book to fruition. I am eternally grateful for FHS Press and Dr. Ben Brotemarkle for taking a chance on publishing my first novel. Thank you, Jon White, for the amazing cover design—couldn't have done it without you. Christine Gallaway, I am indebted to you for your multiple edits along the way and with my finished manuscript —merci! Thanks, Ben DiBiase, for helping me with the back-cover blurb—I was struggling with it and you came to my rescue. Charles Tingley, you were key in my research on the Anhorns and Pinehurst —your help in providing newspaper clippings about Pinehurst and maps to locate the area where the school once existed proved to be invaluable—I thank you. Lynn Palermo, thank you for your classes on the Armchair Genealogist website and your expertise in critiquing my manuscript. I don't think this book would exist without you. To my sister, Jennifer Fitch, thank you for putting up with my requests of reading my manuscript multiple times for clarity and cohesion— and typographical errors! To my husband Steve—I am thankful for your constant support throughout the development of my story and for reading my manuscript many, many times. You offered valuable suggestions during the revision stage which were most helpful. You are my hero.

Author's Note

This book is based on actual people, places, and events. In the case of the main characters and places, real names have been used. The sources for the narrative came from stories my grandfather, Henry, told my mother (who later relayed the story to me) of his time at Pinehurst; a creative story; and newspaper articles which recounted former students' experiences while at the school. While the main characters are the cornerstone of the story, their thoughts, words, and some of their actions are a product of the author's imagination. Minor characters and their thoughts, words, and actions are used fictitiously. The timeline of the story has been altered slightly to tell a more compelling tale.

1

Jacksonville, Florida
Saturday, July 1, 1905

"Henry!" Kate's voice split the silence in the peaceful Jacksonville neighborhood. Standing on the back stoop with hands planted on her hips, she stared at the gray work table just outside the kitchen. The well-worn wooden tabletop was covered with fish entrails, skin, and heads. The stench of rotting flounder filled her nostrils. "Get out here now!" Fuming, her pale complexion flushed. "Henry!" Strands of raven hair clung to her moist brow. Entering the kitchen, she slammed the heavy oak door behind her.

Henry took one step at a time. The wiry eleven-year-old walked down the stairs brushing his disheveled hair out of his eyes. *I wonder what it is this time.* He swung open the kitchen door. Staring at his feet, he mumbled, "Yes, ma'am?"

"Follow me," Kate walked her stepson out to the stoop. "What is this?" She flung out her arm, pointing to the mess.

"Um, fish guts. I cleaned the flounder I caught yesterday so you wouldn't have to. I guess I forgot to clean it up," Henry's voice trailed off.

Kate glared at him. "Who do you think should clean up this mess?" Before he could answer, she said, "It's your responsibility. Clean it up now!" Henry hesitated. "Go on, get busy!"

With his head down, Henry went to the old shed and got a bucket and a hand shovel. Sweat prickled his forehead. He knew it would be another sweltering summer afternoon. Henry braced himself against the odor of rotting guts. The decomposing fish was almost too much; he had to stop and walk away a few times to get some fresh air. Henry noticed there was no hint of a breeze—the still air suffocating and hot. The midday sun baked the mess onto the tabletop. He struggled to pry the sticky remains loose. He filled a larger bucket with fresh water, splashing everywhere as he walked back to the mess. He poured the water on the tabletop and sat down and waited a few minutes, hoping it would help. Kate jerked the door open. "Henry! Why aren't you working? I told you to clean up the mess you made!" Clenching her teeth, her face turned red.

"I'm letting the water soak in, so it'll loosen the fish." *Can't she just let me do this?*

Kate crossed her arms and continued to rant. "Well, hurry up—you don't have all day. You need to go to the grocery store for me when you're done, so back to work!" She spun on her heel and went back inside.

Henry rolled his eyes. He got up and attempted to scrape off the fish. *She's not my Mother!* The more he scraped, the madder he got. *I was being nice to her by cleaning the fish. And this is the way she treats me?* His eyes welled up with tears, making it difficult to see what he was doing. He couldn't believe his father had married someone else. How could he? And to her? He scraped, and the chunks of decaying fish began to yield to his effort. Globs of fish parts fell into the bucket. Henry continued until the tabletop was free of the gooey remains.

At the back of the property he dug a hole, dumped in the decomposing mess, and filled it with dirt. Henry went to the kitchen to get the soap and a brush to finish the job. Ten minutes later, he was sprinting upstairs to the bathroom. Henry drew a cool bath and got in the clawfoot tub, the water refreshing on his hot skin. He scrubbed himself from head to toe with Ivory soap, ridding himself of the fishy odor. Henry dressed in clean clothes and combed his auburn hair.

Walking down the stairs, he almost bumped into his sister, Ruth. "Watch out where you're going!" At thirteen she was tall and lean, with her mother's good looks and her father's blue eyes. Taking two steps at a time, she bounded up the stairs, her dark chocolate hair bouncing on her shoulders.

Ignoring his sister, Henry went the roundabout way to the kitchen. He took the list from the countertop and glanced at the time: three o'clock.

....

Opening the front door, the hot, humid air smacked Henry in the face. He strolled down East First Street and got on the trolley at Main. The streets of downtown Jacksonville were alive with noise and people rushing about, reminding him of ants scurrying around an anthill. He got off at Bay Street and headed east. Henry loved Bay Street: the people hustling and bustling down the sidewalks; the noisy trolleys rumbling down the street; the stores displaying their wares in big windows.

He stopped in front of Cohen's Department Store and gazed at the display. Spotting a brand-new fishing pole, his eyes widened. *Wow! I sure would love to have that!* Knowing he would be late getting home, Henry moved to the next window. He continued to peruse the different stores' displays until he reached the grocery store. Opening the door, the cooler air washed over Henry like a wave. "Hi, Mr. Knaur. Is my dad here?"

"No, Henry, he's at the warehouse getting supplies for the store," Mr. Knaur said. Henry frowned. William Knaur and Herman Conrader had opened the grocery and dry goods store two years before. Henry gave the list to Mr. Knaur, and the older gentleman gathered the items and rang up the groceries.

"See you later, Mr. Knaur," Henry said, jumping down the steps.

....

Kate fussed at him for being late the moment he arrived home. With his back to her, he stuck out his tongue in response. Henry climbed the stairs to his bedroom. Opening the door, he kicked off his shoes and snatched his baseball off the shelf. Flopping down on his twin bed, he tossed the ball up in the air and caught it, each time throwing it higher until it almost touched the ceiling. *What makes her so mean?*

Tick, tick, tick. Seconds clicked by on the small brass alarm clock sitting on Henry's bedside table. Five-fifteen. Henry studied the gold-framed photograph next to the clock. It was his favorite: taken in January 1902, just weeks before his mother died. He gazed at her face and fought back tears. Eleanor's beautiful features were not captured in the sepia-toned photograph. It didn't show her jade-green eyes, nor the sheen of her coffee-bean-colored hair; her delightful smile absent. It didn't matter to Henry. Nothing could erase the image he had of her in his mind.

Thoughts of happier days wandered into Henry's mind. A time when things were good. *Mother never yelled at me the way Kate does.* The memories of his mother were comforting. Sniffing, he stared out the window and watched the storm clouds roll in, turning the beige walls dark. Henry got up and closed the window. Tears welled up in his eyes as the rain began to spatter the glass.

....

Herman Conrader closed the front door and removed his wet raincoat and hat, placing them on the coatrack in the vestibule. Kate stomped out of the kitchen and asked Herman to join her. Herman leaned over to kiss her but she turned away, went to the parlor, and took a seat. Storm clouds hid the sun, darkening the ordinarily cheery room. The stained-glass table lamp did little to lighten the parlor or Kate's sour mood. "Herman, I'm at my wit's end! Henry does the most irresponsible things. This morning, he cleaned the fish he caught yesterday and left a huge mess. You should have seen the table out back. It was full of rotten fish heads and innards! He didn't clean up after himself, and by this afternoon, the stench was sickening. And, if that wasn't enough, he was late getting home from the store!"

"Kate, he just turned eleven, he's still a kid. And besides, it's not like those are criminal offenses." Herman placed a hand on Kate's knee.

Pulling back, she crossed her legs. "You've got to do something. If it's not one thing, it's another with him." Kate's irritation was unmistakable.

Herman took in a deep breath. "I'll talk to him. We've only been married a few months—he needs time to adjust. You know he was just seven when his mother died. Let's not be too hard on him." With a furrowed brow, Kate stood. Without saying a word, she crossed the reception hall and went to the kitchen. *Clank! Bang!* Pots and pans clamored against each other as Kate got busy with supper.

Herman picked up the Florida *Times-Union* newspaper and read, trying to get his mind off the conversation with Kate. His thoughts drifted to Henry as he watched the rain let up. He tried to think of a fitting punishment for the mess Henry made. Deep down, he felt cleaning up the putrid fish was punishment enough. However, to appease Kate, he needed to come up with something more. He stood and opened the front window. The lace curtains billowed in the gentle breeze, the fresh air rolling into the room.

....

Herman knocked on Henry's bedroom door, pushing it open. "Henry? How are you doing?"

Henry sat up and threw his legs over the side of the bed, staring at the floor. "Okay, I guess. Kate's mad at me for making a stinky mess."

"Yes, she's upset. You know the rules around here about cleaning up after yourself. Frankly, I'm surprised you left the fish on the table. What got into you?"

Henry looked up at his father. "Thomas came by and wanted me to go catch frogs with him down at the river's edge. I guess I forgot to clean up."

"Why were you late getting home from the store?"

"I was looking in the store windows and forgot the time."

"You know that when you have a job to do, you need to be responsible and see it through from beginning to end. Do you want to say anything before I decide what your punishment is?"

"No, sir." Henry stared at the floor.

Herman thought for a moment as he stroked his moustache. "Since Thomas was your distraction this morning, you'll not be allowed to visit with him for two weeks."

Henry winced. "Yes, sir." Not being able to spend time with his best friend was the worst punishment his father could give; Thomas was Henry's only escape from Kate's constant nagging and yelling.

....

In preparation for the evening's meal, Ruth folded the napkins and set the table to Kate's specifications. The dining room, decorated in an Asian style, had pale jade green wallpaper with a delicate cherry blossom motif. Noticing the rain had stopped, she slid back the gold silk drapes and ecru lace curtains and opened the windows. The scent of flowers and wet earth replaced the stagnant air. Gazing out the window to the flower garden her mother had planted years ago, Ruth smiled. It was a riot of color with lilacs, hydrangeas, chrysanthemums, and carnations. Baby's breath and larkspur were interspersed throughout. Ruth took over the job of weeding and watering the garden after her mother died. She was determined to care for it the way Eleanor had.

A few minutes before seven, Kate placed the serving dishes on the massive table. The smell of fried fish and freshly baked bread emanated throughout the house. Inspecting the table, she was pleased Ruth had set it to her satisfaction. Kate brought in the last dish and eyed the windows. She closed the lace curtains to help block the view. Kate didn't like the garden; she wanted to replace the unkempt design with a more formal rose garden.

At seven o'clock, Kate called the family to the dining room for supper. She had prepared the flounder Henry had caught, along with potato fritters, green beans, and dinner rolls. Once the family was seated, Kate announced there would be lemon chiffon cake for dessert, to the delight of everyone.

"Everything smells delicious," Herman said. Kate prepared a plate for everyone, giving herself an extra helping of potato fritters. Picking up a piece of flounder, Herman took a bite of the flaky fish. "Why, I believe this is the best I've ever had." He winked at his son. A smile crawled across Henry's face.

Noticing the exchange, the hair on the back of Kate's neck bristled. "Yes, Herman, the fish is delicious. It's too bad Henry had to make such a mess while cleaning them." Her narrowing eyes settled on Henry.

Herman's jaw went slack. "Can we please have a pleasant supper, Kate?"

"Yes, of course." She stabbed at her food.

Henry lowered his head and sank into his seat. He focused on his meal, staring at his food as he ate. *Mother would never say something like that!* He felt his eyes water and he blinked away the moisture. Henry pushed the food around on his plate.

Hoping to lighten the mood, Herman said, "What did you do today, Ruthie?"

"Elizabeth and I went to Riverside Park to feed the ducks. They ate all the bread we had. The ducks went crazy and almost bit off our fingers!"

"You need to be more careful; they say ducks like to eat little girls!" Herman's eyes sparkled.

"Oh, Father! Don't be silly. Ducks don't eat people!"

"Maybe not, but you still need to be cautious." The family settled into an uncomfortable silence; a morose mood persisted throughout the meal. When everyone was finished with supper, Kate and Ruth cleared the china and serving dishes from the table.

Kate walked through the swinging door from the kitchen carrying the family's favorite dessert, the lemon chiffon cake. "Here we go, everyone." Kate placed it on the table.

Herman and Kate made small talk while the family ate the cake. "Oh, Herman, I picked up your brown suit at the tailor's, so you'll have it for church tomorrow."

....

Sunday, July 2, 1905

Dressed in their nicest clothes, Henry, his father, stepmother, and Ruth went to St. John's Episcopal Church. It was only ten-thirty, and the temperature was climbing fast. When the family arrived at the large, wooden structure, Kate went to the ladies room to freshen up. Herman took the children into the sanctuary and found a place to sit.

In the ladies room, Kate opened her purse and removed her handkerchief. She dampened it and pressed it to her face, without much relief. Adjusting her navy-blue skirt, she made sure her crisp white shirt was tucked in neatly. Kate paused and listened in to the other ladies' conversations, trying to hear the latest gossip in Jacksonville. She removed her hat to make sure her hair was in place. A lock of black hair spilled onto her shoulder. Kate pinned it again and replaced her hat. Satisfied, she left and went to find Herman and the children.

Mary Thompson, the church organist, was playing "Praise to the Lord, the Almighty"[1] as Kate entered the sanctuary. Reverend Shields walked to the pulpit, the music fading. He gave a poignant sermon on helping others. Herman closed his eyes and nodded, listening to

1. Joachim Neander, "Praise to the Lord, the Almighty," 1665.

Shields. The inspirational sermon resonated in Kate's ears. Ruth took in each word. Henry listened intently to Reverend Shields. His words stuck in Henry's mind, "Jesus expects us to help others even when we don't want to help them."

....

Pinehurst Collegiate Seminary
St. Johns County, Florida
Sunday, July 2, 1905

Miss Gertrude walked into the large classroom and set her Bible on the podium. Pale white sunbeams streamed in from the four large windows. "Bow your heads and let us recite our opening prayer." The small group did what they were told. Speaking in unison, they prayed.

She lifted her head and gazed at the children. Since it was summertime, there weren't as many children as there were during the school year. Joining the six children were her sister Fannie on the piano, and two field hands who worked at Pinehurst, John and Dan. Miss Gertrude opened her Bible to Proverbs, chapter 3, verses 11 and 12 and read aloud. She closed the Bible and paused. "The Good Book teaches us that discipline and correction are necessary for growth in every aspect of our lives. The older we are the more mature we should be mentally, spiritually and physically. However, there is a danger present in our journey into spiritual maturity—rebelling against discipline and correction. You must submit to His ways of loving. If we are respectful and receive His discipline and correction, we grow up. If we don't, we go backward." Miss Gertrude droned on with the sermon for more than an hour. Finally, she finished, and Miss Fannie played the piano, the group singing "Rock of Ages."[2] "One final remark before dismissal: Remember, submit to the Lord when you are punished and corrected. You must if you are to grow closer to Him. You may go now," Miss Gertrude said.

....

Jacksonville

The family returned home from church and had a hearty meal. After dinner, Henry went to his room and lay on his bed. *Stupid punishment! I wish I could see Thomas today.*

---

2. Reverend Augustus Toplady, "Rock of Ages," 1763.

"Hi," Ruth said to Henry, walking past his bedroom.

"What are you doing?"

Ruth stopped, standing in Henry's bedroom doorway. "I was going to go to Elizabeth's house, but she's got company today. Want to do something?" She went in and sat on the edge of Henry's bed.

"Like what?"

"I don't know. We haven't played King's Castle[3] in a long time. Want to?"

"Sure. You going to get it?" Henry raised his eyebrow.

"Yes, I'll get it. You are so lazy!" She stood and shoved him playfully. Ruth scooted down the stairs and into the parlor to get the game.

The two played most of the afternoon, having a good time. "You know, Mother would have liked this game," Ruth said, with a touch of melancholy in her voice.

"Yeah, I think so, too. Do you still think about her much?"

"A day doesn't go by that I don't think of Mother. I miss her so much."

"Me, too. I don't feel like playing anymore." He put the game pieces back in the box. Ruth's heart ached for him. Henry did not handle his mother's death well; he had gone into a depression and it continued to linger. He flopped back on his bed and crossed his arms.

3. Parker Brothers, "King's Castle," 1902.

2

Jacksonville
Tuesday, July 4, 1905

After breakfast, Herman asked the children if they would like to go to the Fourth of July celebration at Riverside Park. Henry and Ruth cheered in response. Herman's eyes pleaded with Kate. Uncomfortable, she gave in and agreed to go. He picked up Friday's Florida *Times -Union* and read off the activities of the day: live music, a parade, a reading of the Declaration of Independence, a regatta, children's games, fireworks, and lots of food. When everyone was ready, they took the Main Street trolley to Bay Street and then switched to the Park Street trolley.

The family got home late that evening, both happy and tired. Exhausted, Ruth and Henry got cleaned up and went to bed. Herman gazed at Kate with loving eyes. "I appreciate you joining the children and me. I know Henry and Ruth enjoyed having you along."

"I had a good time. It was nice to do something as a family." Herman slept well—the first night in a long time.

....

Pinehurst Seminary
St. Johns County
Tuesday, July 4, 1905

"So much for celebrating the holiday," Dan said, picking the butter bean pods. He threw a handful into a basket, stood and stretched. Taking off his cowboy hat, he wiped his brow with a handkerchief.

"Yes, Suh. I ain' done celebrated since I was a youngun' in Georgia," John said. Twenty years older than Dan, John had worked for the Anhorns going on twenty-five years. He was used to not celebrating much. Gertrude let them have Sundays, Thanksgiving Day, Christmas

Eve, and Christmas Day off. The rest of the days were spent toiling in the fields, working in the barn, or getting caught up with other chores.

....

Jacksonville
Wednesday, July 5, 1905

The brilliant morning sun shone through Henry's window. He lay in bed thinking about Kate and what Reverend Shields had said on Sunday about helping others. Maybe if I'm nice to her she won't be so mean. Henry got up, made his bed, and got dressed. He went downstairs and found Kate cleaning the kitchen. "Would you like some help? I can sweep the floor for you."

"Yes, that's very thoughtful of you. The dining room needs sweeping." Henry got the broom and dustpan. This was one of his favorite rooms in the house; he had many fond memories of family meals with his mother. He opened the lace curtains, and sunlight flooded the room. On the wall opposite the marble fireplace was a cherrywood sideboard with plates, glassware, and Kate's prized collection of chocolatières. The pots, ornate and highly decorated, were her favorite. Each pot, used for hot chocolate, was handmade. All antiques, most had belonged to her grandmother.

Beginning at the far end of the room, Henry saw he'd have to be thorough with his sweeping; it didn't take long for the dust and debris to collect when the windows were open. Henry swept, not missing a spot. Ready to leave the room, he swung around. *Crash!* The broom handle knocked one of the chocolate pots onto the parquet floor, shattering it into a thousand pieces. Kate rushed into the room. "What was that?" Glancing around, her gaze settled on the ceramic pieces strewn over the floor. Her eyes flew open wide, her nostrils flaring.

"I'm sorry. It was one of those pots. It was an accident, the broom handle hit . . ."

"How can you be so careless?" Kate glared at Henry. "It's always something with you, Henry! Go to your room. I'll take care of this." Her caustic tone echoed in his ears.

Henry went to his room and snatched his baseball and lay on his bed tossing it in the air. He replayed the incident over and over in his mind. His chest was filled with an emptiness he was all too familiar with. A tear dribbled out of the corner of his eye. Henry picked up the photograph of his mother and held it to his chest. He curled up into a ball and cried.

....

After finishing her morning duties, and cleaning up the smashed chocolate pot, Kate went to the parlor. She grabbed the paper and flipped through the pages. An advertisement caught her attention. It read:

"Pinehurst Collegiate Seminary at New Switzerland, Fla., for girls and boys, will be accepting students for the new school year in August. Special attention given to orphans. Terms in reach of all. For particulars address Gertrude Anhorn, principal."

When Herman arrived home, he walked to the kitchen to find Kate. He kissed her hello; she pulled back. "Kate, what is it?" In a calm, tired voice, Kate told Herman what happened with the chocolate pot. Herman sighed. He knew something needed to change, but he didn't know what. "Let's go in the parlor where we can talk."

Herman turned on the light, illuminating the robin's-egg blue walls. When they were seated in the two mahogany chairs, Herman said, "I know you think he does things to irritate you, but I don't feel that's the case. I think he's immature and careless. He needs more time to grow up."

"I don't know, Herman. I understand he was devastated when his mother died, but it was more than three years ago. He's no longer seven years old. It's time he takes responsibility for his actions."

"I agree. By age eleven a child should be more responsible, but Henry's had it rough. I think he needs more time."

"How many more years, Herman?" Kate picked up the newspaper from the marble-top table. "I read something interesting in the paper today." She handed it to Herman, opened to the page with the advertisement she had seen earlier. He read the ad. Placing the paper on the table, his posture slumped. Sitting motionless and saying nothing, he stared out the window. "Well, Herman, what do you think?" After a minute of silence, Kate stood and excused herself to the kitchen, her stomach churning.

Herman thought about the ongoing tension between Kate and Henry, and Kate's responses to his actions. He understood her frustrations, but it didn't make things any easier. Herman closed his eyes and rubbed his forehead. After sitting in silence for a while, he went upstairs to change his clothes and freshen up for supper.

....

After a quiet supper, Herman retired to the parlor to finish reading the newspaper. Unable to focus on anything but Kate's wish to send Henry to a boarding school, Herman read the advertisement again. *Am I supposed to choose between Henry and Kate?* He placed the paper on the table, stood, and paced the floor. Herman sat down again, perspiration dotting his forehead. Cradling his head in his hands, his shoulders sank. He extinguished the light and sat in the darkness with only his disconcerted thoughts, the silence pounding in his ears. Hours later, he made his way to the staircase, taking one step at a time, his feet were like lead weights. He changed his clothes and without a sound, slipped between the sheets.

The next morning, Herman got ready for work. While shaving, he saw his reflection in the mirror. A haggard face with dark circles under the eyes stared back at him. Herman rinsed the rest of the shaving soap off, dried his face, and got dressed. Finding Kate in the kitchen, he said in a morose, flat tone, "Go ahead and write to the school for more information." After completing her morning work, Kate penned a letter to the principal of Pinehurst.

3

Wednesday, July 12, 1905

A week later, Kate received the response she was waiting for from the school. She ripped open the envelope, scrutinizing its contents. The letter, from Miss Gertrude Anhorn, painted a lovely picture of Pinehurst Collegiate Seminary: a varied and challenging curriculum, small jobs to teach responsibility, time for exercise and play, Bible study on Sunday mornings, three meals a day, and shared dorm rooms—two children per room. Per-student expenses were two hundred dollars for the school year, or twenty-three dollars a month. Pinehurst also offered a summer program. The letter included a list of required clothing and necessities, and directions. Information about parental visitation was also noted. Children were expected to arrive during the third week of August to be ready for the first day of school on August 21. Kate, pleased with what she read, smiled to herself.

....

Pinehurst Collegiate Seminary
St. Johns County, Florida
Wednesday, July 12, 1905

Gripping the edge of the massive walnut desk, Jack flinched with each strike of the leather strap on his backside. He was determined to not cry out. No, he wasn't going to give her the satisfaction. When she was finished, Jack stood and faced the old woman. "Let that be a lesson to you, Jack. You'd better watch your step. Next time the punishment will be double!" Jack gave her a blank stare then headed out the office door. Miss Gertrude placed the worn strap around her neck.

Fannie Anhorn walked to her sister's office at the front of the aging classroom, passing Jack in the narrow hallway. She sensed that all was not right with the boy. Fannie opened the office door. "Why was Jack here?"

"In trouble again. Third time in less than a month." Miss Gertrude's face was still red with anger.

"Have a heart, Gertrude! The boy has no family and no place else to go. Can't you show him some compassion?"

"Compassion? That urchin doesn't deserve any! He's nothing but a trouble maker—does things just to irritate me. I won't, can't, tolerate that kind of behavior from anyone!" Gertrude stared at Fannie, almost daring her to talk more about this "compassion" nonsense.

Anger boiled up inside Fannie, and she spoke before she thought. "You're just like Father, Gertrude. One misstep from a child, and you punish him, relishing every moment. May God have mercy on your soul."

"I don't need mercy. Father did what he had to do! Children need discipline; without it there is chaos. I don't know why you even care; I'm the one who received the worst of the punishment from Father. You and Minnie had it easy compared to me. Now do us both a favor and get out of my office!" Gertrude's nostrils flared.

Contempt flashed in Fannie's eyes. Gertrude pulled the strap from around her neck and raised her arm, ready to strike Fannie across the back. Fannie was quick; she made it out the door, slamming it behind her. Gertrude's face took on a purplish-red hue. She stomped to her desk and sat, fuming at Fannie's disrespect.

Walking on the sandy path to the dormitory, Jack brushed his black, wavy hair out of his eyes. The fourteen-year-old orphan was used to the punishment the psychopath dished out. Living at Pinehurst for the last six years of his life taught him much about people and what made them tick, except Miss Gertrude. The best he determined was that she was the devil. She was pure evil, through and through.

....

Jacksonville
Thursday, July 13, 1905

After supper, Kate told Herman she had received the information from Pinehurst and wanted to talk to him about it. Herman turned on the light in the parlor. With a stony look on his face, he said, "Well?"

Kate read the letter to Herman. "Traveling there should be fairly easy. We can travel by steamboat; we can take the *Magnolia* to Pinehurst and come home on the *Welaka*."

"I don't know, Kate. Twenty-three dollars a month is no small amount. It sounds like a good place, but I'm not sure."

"Herman, it has everything LaVilla Grammar School has and more. Perhaps he'll learn responsibility there, and it'll help him once he returns home. We can also try it out on a month-to-month basis. We're not required to pay the whole year in advance. If we feel it's not the right place for him, we bring him home. What could possibly go wrong?"

Herman pondered Kate's words. "I don't think he would like to go there by himself. You know how he can be; he doesn't like being alone. I know he'll make friends, but it's not the same as family."

Kate had thought of this and was prepared to respond. "What do you think about sending Ruth to Pinehurst as well?" She bit her lip, unsure how Herman would reply. Minutes went by with no response. She smoothed her skirt, "Herman?"

"Why, Kate? I thought your issues were with Henry, not Ruthie, too."

"No, no, Herman, you misunderstood what I meant. I think it would be easier for him if Ruth was there. Also, I think she would benefit from attending such an excellent school. Please think about it, Herman."

"Okay, Kate, I will. There's still time; we don't need to decide right away."

....

Saturday, July 15, 1905

Tired of being bored, Henry asked permission to go to Thomas's house. His father said yes, and Henry was out the door in a flash. Half walking, half running, he arrived at Thomas's house in no time. Henry

17

knocked on the door and tried to slow his breathing. "Want to go down to the river?" he blurted out when Thomas opened the door.

"Where have you been? I stopped by your house the other day, and your stepmother told me you weren't allowed to come out. What happened?" Thomas's unkempt, sandy-blond hair hung in his eyes.

"I got in trouble, and my punishment was I couldn't see you."

"Let me ask my mother if I can go, and we can talk on the way." Thomas went into the house, leaving Henry on the doorstep. Returning in less than a minute, the two set off for the St. Johns. A year older than Henry, Thomas was tall for twelve. His slight frame and long legs carried him faster than Henry could walk, and he was always a step behind Thomas wherever they went. "So, what did you do this time?" Thomas slowed and looked at Henry.

"You know those flounder we caught a couple of weeks ago?"

"Yeah, I remember, what happened?"

"Well, the next morning, I thought I'd be nice and clean them so Kate wouldn't have to. Then you came along, and I left without cleaning up the mess. That's why I got in trouble."

"Why didn't you ask me to help you? We could've had it done in less than ten minutes."

"I forgot. Playing in the river with you is a lot more fun than cleaning up fish guts."

"You sure are in trouble a lot."

"Yeah, I don't think she likes me. She picks on me all the time." Panting, he tried to keep up as they walked.

"She picks on you. All the time." Thomas smirked.

"She gets mad at me no matter what I do!" The boys slowed to a stop.

Thomas's intense blue eyes stared at Henry. "I know she can be mean sometimes, and she yells a lot, but you're not so innocent."

"What? Sometimes I forget. It's not my fault!" Henry began walking again.

"Okay, okay, you don't need to get mad." They continued on to the river, walking in silence.

Within minutes they had their shoes off, squishing the soft mud between their toes in the cloudy water. They were on the hunt for minnows, but to their disappointment, they weren't able to catch a single one. Thomas suggested they forget about the small fish and race twigs in the current instead. The boys stayed at the river's edge until the sun was hidden by storm clouds.

...

Thursday, July 27, 1905

Kate was getting anxious. Two weeks had passed without a word from Herman about Pinehurst, and time was running out. They had just over two weeks to talk with the children, make preparations, and arrive at the school. Preoccupied with her thoughts, Kate did not hear the front door open. Herman walked in and went straight to the parlor. "Kate, would you please come here?"

"Yes, Herman?" Kate walked into the room, wrinkling her brow.

"Have a seat." Herman rubbed the back of his neck and sat down. Kate smoothed her skirt, sitting down in the other chair.

"What is it? Is something wrong?" Kate clasped her hands.

"No. I've been thinking a lot about sending the children to Pinehurst." Herman inhaled deeply. "Under the current circumstances, I understand why you brought up the idea of sending them to a boarding school. It's not to say making a decision has been easy."

"I know it's been hard on you. But I really think they will do much better at Pinehurst."

Herman looked at Kate with a bit of disdain. "Kate, I know Henry is a problem for you. They can do well at the local school, too."

"I know they'd do well here. But I truly believe that they would excel at Pinehurst. Like I said, it doesn't have to be permanent; we can bring them home anytime."

"The cost is a concern as well. Forty-six dollars a month is quite a bit of money—we'll need to cut back our spending." He hesitated.

"If you're convinced that they will do well, then let's do it. We should speak with them after supper tonight."

"Yes, of course, Herman." Kate stood, a warm feeling flowing through her. She headed back to the kitchen to finish preparing the evening's meal.

....

After supper, Herman called Henry and Ruth into the parlor. "Kate and I would like to talk to you." Herman and Kate sat together on the settee, and the children in the two armchairs. "Summer is coming to a close, and you know what that means—school will begin soon. Kate and I talked, and we found what we think is an exciting opportunity for you. There is a school we would like you both to attend. It's much different than the schools you are used to. The school is called Pinehurst, and it's a boarding school."

Ruth, a little leery, asked, "What's a boarding school?"

"It's a special school—it's where you live at the school. You'll have a room to sleep in, a dining room to eat in, and a schoolhouse to learn in. Everything you need is right there. You don't have to leave the property."

"I don't understand. Why would we do that? We've got a house to live in and a dining room to eat in here."

Herman chuckled. "Yes, we do, Ruthie, but this is different. You'll be able to experience new and exciting things; things you wouldn't be able to do by living at home. You'll meet new friends and learn many interesting things."

Henry listened intently, unsure about this "boarding school." Kate read the letter from Miss Gertrude to help explain the details. "It does sound like a wonderful school," she added.

"Well, it does sound sort of okay," Ruth said. "But I don't know. When would you visit us?"

"Right now, I think every other Sunday would work," Herman answered.

"But it means we won't see you for two weeks at a time!"

"Yes, Ruthie, but I think you'll be enjoying yourselves. The time will fly by. Besides, we can write letters to each other to stay in touch."

"I don't like that, Father. It's a long time."

"We can try it and see how it goes. I think once you are settled in, things will go smoothly, and every other week will work out fine."

"What about Thanksgiving and Christmas?" Henry spoke up.

"I'm not sure about how it'll work with Thanksgiving yet, but you'll be home for two weeks at Christmastime."

"No Thanksgiving?" Henry said, frowning.

"Maybe, maybe not. We'll have to see when the time comes." Herman paused. "Any more questions?"

"How long does it take to get there?" Ruth asked.

"About five hours by steamboat."

Henry perked up. "By steamboat? That would be fun."

"I think you'll enjoy the trip. There's a lot to see on the St. Johns."

Henry was still not convinced this was a good idea. Shifting in his seat, he said, "When would we have to go?"

Kate referred back to the letter. "The third week of August, so in about two and a half weeks."

Henry exhaled and frowned, rubbing his hands together. "I don't know. That's really soon."

Herman checked the time. "It's time for you two to get ready for bed. We need to let Miss Anhorn know right away if you'll be attending, so think about it. The sooner we come to a decision, the better. I'd like to be able to write her tomorrow to let her know if you'll be going or not." Ruth and Henry went upstairs to get ready for bed.

....

"That seemed to go okay," Kate said.

"Yes, I'm a little surprised Henry didn't take it harder. I thought he'd be totally against it. I can't help but think what might happen to us as a family. I don't want us to grow apart."

"Herman, don't be silly. Those kids love you. Nothing's going to change that. If anything, I think it'll draw us closer together."

"I hope you're right. Come on, it's late. Let's go upstairs."

....

Dressed in his nightshirt and ready for bed, Henry knocked on Ruth's door. "Can I come in?" he whispered.

"Yeah."

"What do you think? Is it a good idea? I don't know—I don't want to leave Father for so long," Henry said.

"I know how you feel. It does seem strange leaving home and not seeing them for two weeks at a time. But on the bright side, it does sound like it would be a good place to go, and I like the idea of meeting new friends. Besides, Kate won't be there. Did you think about that?"

"No. That might not be so bad—it sure would be nice to not be in trouble all the time." Henry lingered in her doorway before going to his room and crawling into bed. He thought about this new school, and how it might be a good thing, but still wasn't convinced. His mind raced. *It sure would be nice to not hear Kate yelling at me all the time.* Henry's busy mind kept him awake for hours before he fell asleep.

....

Friday, July 28, 1905

The next morning at breakfast, Herman asked, "Well, Henry, Ruthie? What do you think? Do you want to go to Pinehurst? I think you'd find the opportunity appealing, and one most children don't get to have. Do you have any last-minute questions?"

Ruth spoke up. "I don't have any questions. But I don't know, though. I'll miss being home." She frowned. "On the other hand, it might make school interesting."

Henry, not convinced it was a good idea, stared at his breakfast. He pushed the eggs around on his plate, "Okay, Father. I'll go."

"You don't sound so sure." Herman raised an eyebrow.

"Well, I guess it sounds okay. I wish it weren't so far away. I'm going to miss being at home. I'll miss my old school and Thomas, too."

"I know. You'll make new friends. Probably more than you've got now." Herman winked.

"If you want me to go, I will."

"I would like you to want to go, not because you think it's what we want."

"It's okay, Father. I want to go." He went back to pushing the eggs on his plate.

"Only if you're sure."

"I'm sure."

Right after Herman left for the grocery store, Kate wrote a letter to Gertrude Anhorn letting her know Ruth and Henry would be attending the school. Henry went to his room and lay on his bed. This morning's talk at breakfast tugged at his thoughts. *Why did I agree to go? I don't want to go to some new school.* Henry frowned.

4

Jacksonville
Wednesday, August 16, 1905

Henry opened his eyes and blinked. *Today is the day we leave for Pinehurst.* His stomach fluttered at the thought. Still sleepy, he dragged himself out of bed and went to the bathroom to wash his face. After a hearty breakfast, the family left for the wharf.

Once on the steamboat, Henry and Ruth went exploring. "Be back here before we leave," Kate said, her voice trailing off as they disappeared out of view. Herman joined Kate and took her hand. Kate's eyes met Herman's. "Are you okay, Herman?"

"Yes. It's a little hard for me. This is the first time I'll be away from them." Herman took in the view of the city and reminisced back to the time when Henry was born; Ruth was so excited to have a baby brother. Not wanting to dwell on the memories and become upset, Herman offered Kate his arm. "Let's take a tour of the boat, shall we?" With her hand in the crook of his elbow, they strolled around the lower deck. They went to the upper deck and viewed Jacksonville's waterfront. The last of the passengers boarded, and the captain blew the *Magnolia's* whistle to indicate it was ready to depart.

....

An hour into the trip, the landscape changed. Gone were the wharfs, buildings, and the crowds. What lay before them was the beautiful St. Johns River, a wild place filled with awe-inspiring sights and sounds. Henry and Ruth were on the upper deck, taking it all in, a soft breeze brushing their faces. The river grew wide after leaving Jacksonville, the banks lined with majestic southern live oaks and towering royal palms.

25

One-hundred-fifty-foot bald cypress trees touched the sky. White-tailed deer grazed in a clearing not far from shore, as brightly colored Carolina parakeets screamed overhead. The children were enthralled. Henry hooted, pointing toward the shore; a dozen soft-shelled turtles were sunning themselves on a partially submerged log. Spanish moss hung like mermaid's hair from the branches of the oak and cypress trees, blowing gently in the breeze.

The river narrowed, and the huge limbs of the southern live oaks reached out casting deep shadows across the water. The boat's captain slowed the *Magnolia* to maneuver through the tight quarters. He announced they would arrive at their first stop, Mandarin, in fifteen minutes. They arrived at the platform and several passengers disembarked. The captain announced they would arrive at the next stop, Fruit Cove, in an hour.

A few more passengers disembarked at Fruit Cove, and the boat continued on to the next town, New Switzerland. Herman checked the time: one-thirty. A wave of sadness hit him. This was not what he wanted. He wanted Ruth and Henry with him, but he knew the environment at home was less than ideal.

At two-fifteen, the *Magnolia* slowed and pulled up to the landing at New Switzerland. A wooden plank jutted out from the bank, just beyond an enormous hollowed-out tree. Herman observed a box with the letters U. S. M. attached to the tree. "Hm. I didn't realize there was a post office here. Should make sending and receiving letters easier."

A boatman helped Herman take the trunks off the boat and into a clearing. A large wagon sat under the shade of a laurel oak. Two hulking draft horses nibbled at the sparse patches of grass. A round, old man with white curly hair sat in the wagon waiting, mopping his brow with a handkerchief. "Afternoon, suh," said the old man. "You mus' be Mister Conrader. And these two mus' be Master Henry and Miss Ruth. My name's Mr. John, and I be taking you to Pinehurs'." He climbed down from the wagon.

"Yes, nice to meet you, Mr. John. This is my wife, Mrs. Conrader."

"My pleasure, Missus Conrader. Here, le' me load them trunks." Mr. John hefted the trunks onto the wagon, then helped Kate and the youngsters board. "Y'all ready?" He returned to the driver's seat.

"I believe so," Herman said.

....

The old man gave two clicks of his tongue and slapped the reins on the horses' rumps. "C'mon, Ajax. C'mon, Apollo, les' go." The horses got their footing and pulled against the weight of the wagon. Mr. John guided Ajax and Apollo out of the clearing and onto a sandy trail. With barely enough room for the horses and wagon, the oak trees surrounded them like a cocoon. "It's abou' a half-hour trip to the school, so we should be there by three o'clock."

"Does anyone else live around here?"

"Naw sir, Mister Conrader. Pinehurs' in the middle of nowhere." Mr. John chuckled. "Closes' neighbor is four mile away."

The dense, overarching oaks thinned out, and a forest of slash pines towered above them, the understory chock-full of palmettos, the sandy ground littered with pine cones. Muscadine grapevines scaled the trees, showing off their dark purple clusters of fruit. Squirrels chattered at the visitors from their perch on a branch. "The sky be cloudin' up. Hope we can ge' you folk inside before the rain come." Ajax and Apollo, now at a steady pace, plodded along. *Smack!* Ajax swatted at flies with his tail. Mr. John, a cheerful fellow, loved to sing. On their way to Pinehurst, he sang "The Cat Came Back."[1]

Kate noticed Herman was in another world. "What's wrong, Herman?"

"I still don't know about this place. The school is so far away from civilization, and it makes me uncomfortable. There's nothing out here but trees and bushes for miles! What do they do in case of emergencies?" Herman whispered.

"We can ask Miss Anhorn. I'm sure she'll answer all our questions."

"I certainly hope so."

The wagon came to a crossroad, and Mr. John pulled the horses to a stop. He pointed to the right. "The Richardsons live three miles south of here. They're the closes' neighbors." The trees and underbrush formed an impenetrable wall.

....

---

1. Harry S. Miller, "The Cat Came Back," 1893.

Ten minutes later, a structure appeared through the forest of trees. Drawing closer, they viewed a large building at the head of a circular drive. A rickety picket fence encircled the building, its gate wide open. An ominous sight, built of pinewood clapboards painted white, the dingy schoolhouse stood in front of them. The belfry, perched on its roof, contained a tarnished brass bell. Staring at the school, Henry saw a figure in the window, the grime on the glass obscuring its identity. A chill slinked down his spine. *This is where we'll go? It's so creepy!* He clenched his jaw; his heart rate quickened. *Something doesn't seem right. I don't want to be here! I want to go home!* Henry broke out in a cold sweat, jumping at the sound of barking dogs.

As they pulled up to the gate, a pack of noisy dogs trotted up to greet the newcomers. "Go on, now, ge' ou' the way. Oh, these dogs. They's friendly, but they sure can be pesky." Mr. John chuckled.

"I think they're adorable," Ruth giggled. "What are their names?"

"There's so many of 'em, I can' remember." Mr. John laughed, his belly jiggling. "I jus' call 'em, 'Hey You!'"

The door to the school opened, and out walked a woman dressed in a tan buttoned-down skirt with a pristine white blouse. Her salt-and-pepper hair was pulled into a bun on top of her head, her face scored with deep frown lines. "Hello, I'm Gertrude Anhorn, the principal. Welcome to Pinehurst. I prefer to be called 'Miss Gertrude,'" she said, her voice sounding like gravel rolling down a hill. She shooed the dogs away.

"Hello, Miss Gertrude, I'm Herman Conrader, and this is my wife, Kate. This is my daughter, Ruth, and my son, Henry."

"I'm pleased to meet you all. Won't you come in?" Miss Gertrude called for Mr. Dan to help Mr. John take the trunks inside. She looked at Henry and Ruth. "We'll get you two settled later; right now I'd like to show you around." As they were walking up the steps of the porch, fat raindrops began to pound the ground. Within seconds, the drops turned into a downpour. "We'll begin here at the schoolhouse. The school and dormitory were built in 1889." The front door opened into a reception hall, with the classroom on the left. Miss Gertrude opened the two massive pocket doors to reveal an oversized room with pale yellow walls and four enormous windows. "This is where the learning takes place." Miss Gertrude fanned her arm in a partial arc. "Each student has his own desk and, as you can see, we have plenty of space."

She drew the family's attention to the front. "My office is through that door." Miss Gertrude pointed to the back. "At the rear of the classroom, we have a piano. The teacher, who is also my sister, uses it to teach the children songs."

They crossed the hall to the next room. A musty smell hung in the air like smoke from a chimney on a still night. Although lit with kerosene lamps, the library remained dim. The faded moss-green walls and the well-worn furniture showed their years of use. Aging bookshelves lined the far wall. Thick velvet drapes blocked all but a sliver of light entering the lone window, which looked out onto the porch. "This is our library with seating and tables for the students. They can use the room to study, write letters, and visit with each other."

"Looks pretty eerie to me," Henry whispered to Ruth.

They visited the dining hall next. Miss Gertrude slid the pocket doors open to reveal a spacious room; its cream-colored walls unadorned. A long oak table stood in the middle, flanked by benches. "Each side can seat ten children." A single chair sat at the head of the table. Raindrops spattered the three windows on the far side. The plank flooring, rubbed smooth by the footsteps of many, was spotless. "The boys sit on this side, and the girls sit on the opposite side. This way to the kitchen."

Miss Gertrude pushed open the door. The smell of dinner hung in the air, greeting the visitors with the aroma of fried chicken. The spotless room was furnished with two cast-iron stoves, two iceboxes, and a double sink. A sizable work table sat in the center. "With the help of my sister, Minnie, and the housekeeper, Miss Nellie, we can easily serve sixty meals a day."

"That's impressive," Kate said, inspecting the room.

"Yes, we do keep busy around here, especially when it's meal time," Miss Gertrude responded, her expression flat.

She led the family out the back door. "This is the students' garden. Each child is assigned a portion to take care of. They do the planting and watering, and eventual harvesting of the food." Miss Gertrude checked the sky. "The rain has let up. We'll continue on to the dormitory." A short distance from the back of the school stood a two-story building. "My invalid father, two sisters, and I live downstairs. The children's rooms are located upstairs. Please, follow me." The small group dodged the mud puddles on the path. A large oak towered above them; water drops fell from the leaves, spattering the visitors as they walked to the entrance.

Opposite the front door was the staircase to the dorm rooms. Miss Gertrude paused on the landing and explained that the girls' rooms were on the right, boys' rooms on the left, and each side had a shared bathroom. She took a left, went to the third door, and stopped. "This room is empty right now, but you'll see how they are arranged. All are the same." She opened the door and stepped aside.

Herman's head jerked back; his muscles went rigid. The room was bleak, its white walls plain and cold. At a mere eight-by-ten feet, it was cramped. Furnished with two cots, a table with a lamp, and two small closets, there was little extra space. Above the table was a window covered with thin curtains and wrought-iron bars. The smell of kerosene permeated the air. He was expecting something larger and more comfortable, and windows without bars. Herman's chest tightened. *I'm leaving my children here?*

Miss Gertrude saw Herman's face, recognizing his expression; it was the same as other parents' faces of first-time students. "Yes, Mr. Conrader, the rooms are small. The children will spend little time here, using them only for sleeping. The bars are for their protection. We wouldn't want someone to fall out of a window, now, would we?" Her right eyebrow shot up.

"No, no, of course not. I was expecting something larger, but your explanation makes sense." Miss Gertrude led them back to the staircase. "It's more like a jail cell than a dorm room," Herman whispered to Kate as he glanced over his shoulder at Henry and Ruth.

Although the rain had stopped, the sky remained dark with storm clouds. The group returned to the schoolhouse and went into the library. Miss Gertrude finished up the tour by telling them about the use of the bell to indicate the time. She stressed the importance of being on time for class, meals, and bedtime. She handed Henry and Ruth a piece of paper detailing what each strike of the bell meant. She focused her attention on Ruth and Henry. "In the mornings, there will be a knock on your door at six-thirty to awaken you so you can be ready for the day. Do you have any questions?" Henry and Ruth, overwhelmed, shook their heads. She turned to Herman and tilted her head.

"Yes, I do. Why haven't we seen any other children?"

"We have a few on campus now, and the rest will arrive over the next three days. We like to space the arrivals out so we can give families a more personalized tour."

"With being so isolated, I want to know how you handle emergencies."

"We have few, if any, emergencies at Pinehurst, Mr. Conrader. We're equipped to handle most issues. If, for any reason, a child needs to visit a doctor, we take him to Fruit Cove, which is about an hour and a half north of here. Of course, we notify the parents immediately if a child needs medical care."

"I see. Thank you, Miss Gertrude." Herman checked his watch: four-twenty. "We need to be at the landing at five o'clock, so we should leave soon." Herman gave Ruth a hug and a kiss on the cheek. "I love you, Ruthie."

He walked over to Henry, who stood staring at the floor. Time slowed for Henry and everything felt surreal. I can't believe they're leaving. A sheen of perspiration covered Henry's face.

"Son, know I love you and will think about you every day." Henry, with a trembling chin and tears in his eyes, hugged his father. He held on, not letting Herman go. "It's time for Kate and me to go, son. We'll visit you in a week and a half, and we can write letters to each other as much as you like." Henry nodded and loosened his grip.

"Bye, Father. I'll miss you. Please write every day!" Ruth choked back tears, smiling the best she could. She walked to Kate and gave her a hug. "Bye, I'll miss you too."

Henry walked to Kate and gave her an uneasy hug. "Bye."

Kate put a hand on Henry's shoulder and lifted his chin with her finger. "I do hope you enjoy your time here."

"I'll try." A tear rolled down his cheek, his lips trembling.

Miss Gertrude pulled the drapes open. "Mr. John is ready to take you to the landing. We'll be in touch."

Herman gave them one last hug before leaving. He helped Kate into the wagon. "I sure will miss those two." Herman's body sagged. Mr. John slapped Ajax and Apollo with the reins. The horses grunted and huffed as they got their footing. Midway down the drive, Herman looked back and surveyed the sky. Clouds cast murky shadows over the schoolhouse.

....

Once aboard the *Welaka*, Herman and Kate settled in the saloon. Sitting in silence, they ate the sandwiches Kate had prepared for the trip home. Herman cleared his throat. "Pinehurst does appear to be a good place, but I can't shake this nagging feeling that something isn't right. I'm still not convinced they can handle emergencies."

"Miss Gertrude has been running Pinehurst for many years. I'm sure she knows what she is doing. As far as sensing something isn't right, I think it's the newness of it all. After all, you said this is the first time you'll be without them. You just have the jitters." The tangerine-tinted sky showcased the deep purple clouds in the west, the reflection dancing off the water. "Isn't it beautiful, Herman?"

"Yes, it is. Too bad the beauty lasts only a short time. Let's go up on the upper deck in the bow and take in the view of the river."

5

Miss Gertrude told Mr. John and Mr. Dan to take Henry's trunk to room number four and Ruth's to number nine. Henry, still in a daze, entered the room after the men deposited the trunk on his cot. To his surprise, there was a boy on the other cot reading.

"Hi, I'm Sammy," the boy said, putting down his book. "I guess we'll be roommates." Sammy was taller and heavier than Henry and strained the cot on which he lay. "You been crying?" His greasy yellow hair almost covered his brown eyes. Grunting, he sat up.

"Yeah, my father and stepmother left a little while ago. My name is Henry. This is my first time here." He sniffed and wiped his red eyes with the back of his hand. "You been here long?" Henry sat down on his cot.

"I got here yesterday, but this is my second year at Pinehurst."

"So, what's it like? Is it okay here? Do you like it?"

"It's like most schools. We learn reading, arithmetic, history, you know, the regular stuff. We also learn about a lot of different things, so it isn't too boring. I'm from Palatka. Where are you from?"

"Jacksonville. Sure is different here. I'm used to lots of people and big buildings, not the woods. Everything's so cut off here. Does that bother you?"

"It did at first, but you'll get used to it. It's kinda nice. There's a lot of wild animals around here."

"Really? What kind?"

33

"Deer, tortoises, birds. Lots of birds. Bobcats too. Some say there are panthers around here."

"Panthers? I've never seen a panther!" Henry's eyes went wide.

"As far as liking it here, it's got its good parts and bad parts."

"What do you mean by 'bad parts?'" Henry's stomach quavered.

"We all got jobs, and they're not much fun. It's work, plain and simple. They assign us jobs based on our age. Your job will probably be with the farm animals."

"That doesn't sound so bad."

"It's not if you like to work. And that's only part of it. They make us work out in the fields too."

"Why?"

"Pinehurst is also a big farm. They use us kids to help plant crops and then harvest them when they are ready."

"Gosh! That sounds like a lot of work."

"It is."

Clang. Clang. The old brass bell rang. Henry fumbled with the paper Miss Gertrude had given him, trying to decipher the meaning of the two chimes.

"It's time for supper. We better go now; we don't want to be late." Sammy stood, tucking his shirt in.

They arrived in the dining hall to find others already seated, a glass of water at each place. The enticing aroma of the food made Henry hungry. They slid onto a bench. The kitchen door swung open, and Miss Nellie, the house servant, delivered the plates to the table. When Sammy saw the ham slices and mashed potatoes, he grinned.

Ruth came in and sat at the end of the table. She was able to catch Henry's eye and gave him a weak smile. His eyes brightened for a moment, but his expression was lost to his overpowering sadness.

Miss Gertrude came out of the kitchen with a short, stout woman and introduced her as her sister, Miss Minnie. She nodded her head and said hello before returning to the kitchen. Miss Gertrude took the seat at the head of the table. "There is to be no talking during meal times," she said, eyeing each child. "Bow your heads." Miss Gertrude said grace, and the children ate. The only sounds were the clinking of forks on plates and the occasional sniff.

After supper Ruth and Henry went to the empty library. The dark, gloomy room mirrored Henry's emotions. "It sure is dark in here," Ruth said, turning up the kerosene lamps. They browsed the many books lining the shelves. After a few minutes, Ruth picked out a book. "This looks interesting. It's called *The Enchanted Island of Yew*.[1] I think I'll read this one."

Henry was unable to focus on choosing a book. "I can't find one. Can you help?" The two scanned the titles hoping to find an intriguing book. Ruth pulled one off the shelf and handed it to him. He read the title: *The Story of King Arthur and His Knights*.[2] "This sounds okay." He sat down and stared at the cover.

"It would be easier to read if you opened it," Ruth giggled, trying to lighten Henry's mood.

"Yeah, I will. I miss Father already. I can't believe we're here. I feel so lonely." A tear ran down his cheek, dangling on his chin before falling on his shirt.

"I miss Father, too. We've got each other; we don't need to be lonely."

"I know. It's so different here, though." Henry flipped through the pages of the book. "My roommate is already here. His name is Sammy, and he told me we all have jobs, and that we have to plant and harvest crops. It sounds like a lot of work; I don't remember Kate saying anything about hard jobs."

"Maybe he was talking about the garden."

"I don't think so. Sammy said our jobs are based on our age, and I'd probably be working with farm animals. Doesn't sound too bad, but with planting and harvesting crops, it sounds like more work than what we're supposed to have."

"He might be stretching the truth. I'm sure Miss Gertrude will tell us all we need to know."

1. Frank L. Baum, *The Enchanted Island of Yew,* 1903.
2. Howard Pyle, *The Story of King Arthur and His Knights,* 1903.

"Are you staying in here to read for a while?"

"Yes, if you are."

They sat in the library reading, the silence interrupted by Henry's sniffing. Finally, Henry stood and said, "I want to go to the dorm and unpack. See you tomorrow."

"Okay, sleep tight." She gave Henry a hug.

....

Henry opened his trunk and put his clothes in the closet. He took out the photograph of his mother. The dim light did not allow him to see her clearly. *I wish you were here, Mother.* Henry traced her face with his finger, his eyes roaming over the picture examining every detail he had memorized. He placed it in his trunk with care. *Clang.* Henry jumped. Sammy laughed and said. "The eight-thirty bell—means we've got thirty minutes until lights out."

"Oh, okay." Henry lay down on his cot; the odor of the clean sheets was somewhat comforting. He told his new roommate good night, and Sammy put out the light; the room, cast into blackness, was unsettling. Henry was tired, his eyes heavy. A shiver crawled down his spine before he fell into a dreamless sleep.

....

Thursday, August 17, 1905

Henry was awakened by a knock on the door. "Ugh. What time is it?"

Sammy sat up and wiped the sleep out of his eyes. "Six-thirty, our wake-up time every morning. It gives us time to wash our faces, eat breakfast, do our jobs, and be on time for school. On Saturday, the same thing, except sometimes we got extra work to do. On Sundays, we go to the classroom for Bible study." He yawned.

"I'm not used to getting up this early. When do we find out about our jobs?"

"Once everyone is here, probably Saturday. We need to make our beds, get dressed, and wash up. Come on, let's go."

Henry smoothed out the white sheets as best he could, then placed the olive-drab wool coverlet on top. He finished by placing the pillow at the head of the bed. They dressed and washed their hands and faces. *Clang. Clang.* Sammy said to Henry, "We have fifteen minutes until we're supposed to be seated at the table." They scooted down the stairs and up the path to the schoolhouse. Just as the boys sat on the bench, Ruth and another girl walked into the dining hall. Henry was struck by the dainty girl's blond hair; it was as light as the morning sun and flowed down her back. Ruth introduced her roommate, Lorene. Henry introduced Sammy to the girls.

Miss Nellie brought in the breakfast plates and served the children. At twenty-five, her dark hair was graying. The burden of a heavy workload for the past few years at Pinehurst had taken its toll on her both physically and mentally.

This morning's fare was pancakes. Miss Gertrude gave thanks and reminded them there was to be no talking. Henry poured syrup over the pancakes and mushed them around his plate. Sammy wasted no time and dug in. With his mouth full, he whispered to Henry, "What are you doing to your food?" He shot a glance at Miss Gertrude.

"I don't like pancakes," he whispered, scrunching up his nose.

"You need to eat. When we start working, you'll be hungry if you don't. We're not allowed to eat between meals." Henry acknowledged him and then took a small bite. He continued until he had eaten half of the pancakes.

"Ugh. I can't eat anymore," he mouthed, almost gagging.

Miss Gertrude walked up to Henry and Sammy. Fearing she had heard them talking, Henry's stomach rolled. "Sammy, why don't you show Henry and Ruth around the grounds?"

"Yes, Miss Gertrude."

"May Lorene come with us, too?" Ruth asked.

"Yes. Be back here in an hour."

"Yes, ma'am."

The four walked out the back door of the schoolhouse, past the garden and the chicken coop. "Where are we going?" asked Henry.

"We'll start with the barn." They walked by the dorm and past a small dwelling. Sammy pointed to the four-room shack; the once dark brown paint now faded. "Mr. John and Mr. Dan live there. Mr. John is the one who picked you up in the wagon, and Mr. Dan is the other field hand who works here." The weathered barn, its metal roof rusty with age, had a weather vane permanently pointing south. To the far right of the barn was the pig sty. Grunting, Sammy slid the enormous barn door open. *Screeech*, it protested under his efforts. Sunshine poured into the barn, illuminating the cobwebs and dust motes floating in the air. A tabby cat lay in the aisle, tapping his tail. Bothered by the visitors, he scampered into a stall and out the window. The smell of horse and cow urine caught the three newcomers by surprise. Henry slapped his hand over his nose and mouth.

"Whew! What is that smell?" Lorene pinched her nose.

"It's so stinky!" Ruth complained.

Sammy laughed. "Welcome to the farm. You got horses and cows in here. They don't got a bathroom, so they use their stalls. The stalls are cleaned every day. Right now, Mr. John and Mr. Dan do it. Soon, it'll be one of us."

"What do you mean, 'one of us?'" Ruth asked.

"We all have jobs on the farm. There are lots of things that need to be done around here, and someone has to do it. So, Miss Gertrude has the kids do chores—cleaning the stalls is one of 'em."

"I hope I'm not the one to do it!" Lorene said.

The barn housed Ajax, Apollo, and two smaller horses, Zippy and Chance. Sammy pointed out the four dairy cows, naming them. "Mr. Dan should be here any minute to put them out to pasture."

A shadow skittered across their path. "Eek! What was that?" Ruth jumped back.

"Ha ha. It's only a mouse. They're all over the place. They like to eat the grain the cows and horses drop. There's a lot of cats in here, too. They eat the mice."

"Yuck! Let's hurry up." Ruth headed for the door.

They walked into the bright sunshine. Things seem different today than they did yesterday, Henry thought. Maybe it won't be so bad.

Sammy shut the cumbersome door, and they continued their walk behind the barn. They passed a fenced-in pasture and two old sheds. Their peeling red paint exposed the gray wood underneath. Pointing to them, Sammy said, "They keep the farm equipment there." Beyond the dilapidated buildings was a field with rows of corn plants swaying in the breeze.

They proceeded to the woods. The wind, filled with the sharp scent of pine, whistled through the needles on the trees. Dark caramel-colored pine needles and soft sand padded the ground, muffling their footsteps. Following the trail deeper into the woods, a gentle breeze rustled the fronds of the saw palmettos crowding the landscape.

Ruth noticed there were big V-shaped cuts on the trees, and buckets attached to most of them. "What are the buckets for?"

"They catch the sap that drips out of the tree. Mr. John and Mr. Dan make turpentine with it for use around the farm. Miss Gertrude uses it as a medicine for cuts and other stuff."

Continuing their walk, Henry eyed big holes at the edge of the trail. "What made this hole?"

"A gopher tortoise. That's its burrow." They continued to the third side trail. Fifty yards in, the vegetation began to change. The pine trees thinned out and were soon replaced by stately water oaks, red maples and cabbage palms. Dead leaves cushioned their steps on the winding path. The high-pitched sound of a thousand cicadas vibrated in their ears. A few minutes later they reached a creek, its lazy current almost motionless. The smell of damp earth floated in the air. "Over there!" Sammy whispered, pointing to a clearing on the opposite side of the creek. Five white-tailed deer grazed on tender plant leaves among the detritus.

"Wow, I've never seen them this close before," Ruth said in a hushed voice. Two of the deer stopped grazing and raised their heads. Without warning, the deer bounded away and were gone in a flash.

"This creek goes into the St. Johns River," Sammy said.

"Any fish in it?" Henry peered into the rust-colored water.

"Nothin' very big. The best fish are caught in the river. Sometimes Mr. John takes a few boys to the river to catch fish for supper. It's fun—maybe you could go sometime. We should head back now. Miss Gertrude will be mad if we're late."

....

When they returned, Miss Gertrude was giving a tour for new parents. Three girls and a boy followed close behind. "Looks like she's hooked four more." Sammy shook his head. Henry, Ruth, and Lorene gave each other puzzled looks.

"I think I'll get my book and read in the library," Henry said. "Anyone else want to go?"

"I'll go with you," Ruth said.

Once in the library, they opened their books to read. Henry couldn't concentrate. "What do you think Sammy meant when he said, 'She's hooked four more?'"

"I don't know. I thought it was sort of strange."

The two went back to their reading. Captivated, they didn't move until the bell rang twice. "What time is it?"

Ruth looked past Henry to the grandfather clock. "Fifteen minutes to twelve. It's almost dinnertime. I wonder what they'll have."

....

Miss Nellie brought in plates with ham sandwiches and apples. Henry eyed the sandwich. *Yum.* One of the new boys sat next to him. "Hi, I'm Henry, what's your name?" he asked.

"I'm Alex Johnsen. Are you new to this place?"

"Yeah, my sister and I got here yesterday." Henry sniffed.

Miss Gertrude took her place at the head of the table. The children bowed their heads, and she gave thanks. "There's to be no talking during meal times."

6

Friday, August 18, 1905

Mr. John pulled up in the wagon with a new student and her parents. He unloaded the girl's trunk, placing it on the porch. Miss Gertrude opened the door and greeted her and her parents. "Hello, I'm Miss Gertrude, the principal here at Pinehurst. You must be Mr. and Mrs. Conner, and this must be Frances. Pleased to meet you. I'd like to show you around."

Twenty minutes later, a carriage bounced its way up the circular drive. Two boys jumped down from the back seat. Sammy walked up and sat next to Henry on the porch steps. "Well, if it ain't David and Eddy Bingham. They were here last year. David must be about eight or nine now, and I think Eddy is two years older. You should've seen 'em when they got here last year. Boy, were they scared." Sammy chuckled.

"Scared? Why were they scared?" Henry furrowed his brow.

"They were young and didn't know any better."

"What do you mean?"

Sammy didn't want to upset Henry. "I'll tell you later." He stood and stretched. The sound of rolling thunder rumbled in the distance. The winds whipped up, and Sammy glanced at the foreboding sky. Raindrops pelted the ground. "We better go in before it gets worse." The boys walked into the library; the musty smell of aging books permeating the air. Sammy pulled out a deck of cards and glanced around. He whispered, "Can't let Miss Gertrude see these. She'll take 'em and burn 'em!"

"Then you should put them away!"

"Where's your sense of adventure? Anyway, she's busy right now with that new girl's parents. Here, I'll teach you a game called slaps. It's fun; I think you'll like it." Sammy sat across from Henry.

"Okay, I'll do it. But let's keep an eye out for her. I wouldn't want you to lose your cards." They managed to play two hands before they heard Miss Gertrude's deliberate footsteps and her thunderous voice barking out instructions to Miss Nellie. "Grab them, quick!" Henry blurted out. Sammy smiled. He gathered the cards and shoved them in his pocket.

"She won't catch me." Moments later, the bell rang twice. "Suppertime." Sammy stood. "I'm hungry, let's go eat."

Afterward, the children gathered in the library and chatted. The new arrivals picked out books to read. Sammy and the "old-timers"were huddled in the corner speaking in hushed voices, occasionally looking over at the new arrivals. Henry glanced over at the group. His interest aroused, he strained to hear what they were saying. The buzz of conversation and quiet sobs drowned the old-timers' voices.

....

Not as tired as the night before, Henry lay awake for what felt like hours. The deafening silence echoed in his ears. *I miss Father.* The deafening quiet was broken by what Henry thought was someone crying. He listened closely but wasn't sure what he heard. Sure sounds like somebody's upset. Henry eavesdropped for a while but heard no more. He went to sleep only to be tormented by nightmares.

....

Saturday, August 19, 1905

At breakfast, Henry sat on the bench next to Sammy. The aroma of bacon drifted in from the kitchen. "It sounded like someone was crying last night," Henry said.

"I'm not surprised. It happens a lot here," Sammy said.

"Who do you think it was?"

"Don't know. Probably one of the new kids." Henry eyed the bacon and eggs Miss Nellie placed in front of him. His mouth watered.

"Yummy!" whispered Henry. Sammy wasted no time and shoved a forkful of scrambled eggs in his mouth.

....

After the noon meal, and after the last group of parents departed, Miss Gertrude called the children into the classroom. "You'll have certain responsibilities here at Pinehurst. Jobs are based on your age. Those who were here last year will help the new students learn their jobs, and then Mr. John and Mr. Dan will teach new jobs to the older children." Miss Gertrude rattled on, "The jobs include cleaning stalls, feeding and watering the horses and cows, collecting sap from pine trees, feeding and watering pigs, housekeeping, feeding and watering the chickens,and gathering eggs, kitchen duty, and milking the cows. Some jobs are done once a day, others twice a day."

Henry stared at his folded hands. *These aren't the kinds of jobs I thought we'd have.* Focused on his thoughts, he didn't hear what Miss Gertrude said next.

"Henry, did you hear me?"

"Um, no, ma'am." He squirmed.

"These are your daily jobs to be completed in the morning after breakfast and/or late afternoons," she repeated.

"Yes, ma'am." Henry swallowed.

Miss Gertrude rattled off the list of names and the jobs each child had. Henry chewed his fingernails until he heard his name called. "Henry and Eddy, you'll feed and water the cows and horses."

He stopped biting his nails. *Doesn't sound too bad.* Henry watched Eddy slide down in his seat and roll his eyes.

Miss Gertrude finished up the boys' list. "Jack, Will, and Sammy, your job is cleaning stalls, which is done right after you finish in the classroom."

Sammy's shoulders slumped. "The worst job on the farm," he whispered to Henry.

Miss Gertrude began assigning the easiest jobs to the younger girls first. Biting her lower lip, Ruth listened to Miss Gertrude read from the list of jobs. "Ruth, Lorene, and Mary, your job is housekeeping. Miss Nellie will tell you more about what it entails."

Ruth mouthed, "How bad could it be?" Lorene shrugged, raising her eyebrows.

Miss Gertrude continued, "It's important that you know your job entails accuracy and skill. You must listen carefully to whomever is teaching you your job. And it's crucial that you do your job in a timely manner." She made eye contact with each of the new students. "Now that you know your individual jobs, you all will also be responsible for a plot in the kitchen garden. You'll sow seeds, water your plants, and pull weeds. You'll harvest the vegetables when they are ripe. Miss Fannie is in charge of gardening, so any questions about the garden need to be directed to her." Miss Gertrude paused to let her words sink in.

"You have no doubt seen quite a few dogs here at the school. They are here for a reason. You'll each be responsible for your own dog. You'll feed and water him, play with him, take him on walks, and brush him. Those of you who were here last year will keep the same dog. The new children will choose a dog for themselves. Some already have names, and some do not. If the dog isn't already named, you may call him whatever you wish. You may take the dog anywhere you like except the school building and the dormitory." This announcement brought squeals of joy from the children. "Mr. John is rounding them up now. He'll bring them out front in a moment."

A slender woman with graying hair walked into the classroom. Dressed in a floor-length brown skirt and a cream-colored blouse with long sleeves, she walked to the front of the classroom. Miss Gertrude said, "This is my sister, Miss Fannie, the teacher."

Miss Fannie was younger than Miss Gertrude by three years, yet she appeared much older than her thirty-seven years. The age hung on her face like a well-worn shoe, deep lines creasing her face. Her tired eyes scanned the children's faces. Miss Fannie adjusted her glasses. "I look forward to working with you; to watch you grow academically, as well as socially. I recognize a few faces. How are you, Eddy? And Sammy? Ruby? And the rest of my old friends. I see many new faces, too. I'm excited to get to know you and help you reach your full potential. Be ready bright and early on Monday morning!" Her soft voice was refreshing.

"Thank you, Miss Fannie. Sounds like Mr. John is out front with the dogs."

Mr. John brought the dogs inside the picket fence and closed the gate. The children scooted out the front door. To their delight, there were dogs everywhere. The returning students quickly found their dogs and went to them. The new students scanned the pack and looked for one to call their own. Lorene found a black dog with a white tip on its tail. She asked Miss Fannie, "May I have her?"

"Yes, she's yours. She doesn't have a name yet."

"Yippee!" Lorene was thrilled. She thought for a moment. "I'm going to call her Tippy!"

Henry found a brindle puppy who was all mutt with a hint of bulldog. "Does he have a name?"

"No, he doesn't. You can call him whatever name you wish," Miss Fannie said. Henry was ecstatic; this was his first dog, and he got to name him. All kinds of names went through his head. He watched the puppy for a couple of minutes and decided on Buster. Henry sat down. The puppy climbed into his lap. Reaching his head up, he slobbered all over Henry's face. He laughed and petted the puppy, enjoying every minute.

Ruth was overwhelmed at her choices and couldn't decide. An older dog, a tan Labrador mix with a white muzzle, walked up to her and started licking her hand. "Oh, how sweet."

"I think she's chosen you." Miss Fannie said.

"What's her name?"

"Her name is Bella. She likes you."

"Can she be mine?"

"I think you two will make an excellent pair."

Eddy walked up to Henry and said, "Hi, I'm Eddy. I guess we'll be working together in the barn feeding the animals." The same age as Henry, Eddy was small for his age. His short red hair complemented his fair complexion and freckles. They chatted until the two spinster sisters told them to go back inside.

When they were gathered in the classroom, Miss Gertrude said, "The dogs are allowed to roam free during the day. They must be put up in the fenced-in area where they can get to their kennels at night," she said, pointing to the north side of the school. "Are there any questions?" The room was silent. "There's still time before supper for you to learn your jobs. If you were here last year, please come to the front of the room." Miss Gertrude paired the experienced children with the new arrivals. "Mr. John and Mr. Dan will assist those of you who do not have a helper. We'll meet by the garden when the supper bell rings so we can show you how to feed the dogs properly."

....

The children headed to their assigned areas. Jack tugged on the weather-beaten door at the front of the barn until it opened. Henry and Eddy followed him inside. Jack, at fourteen, was the oldest student at Pinehurst. Tanned and stocky, he demonstrated how to feed the animals the grain, then went to the hayloft and showed how much to give each animal. Jack grabbed two buckets and took Henry and Eddy outside to the well. He pumped the handle until the water flowed freely, stopping when the water filled the buckets halfway. "Don't fill 'em any more than this or you won't be able to carry them." He picked up the buckets with ease.

Jack showed them how to open the stall door and have the animal step back while pouring the water in the trough. He emphasized how important it was to make the animals back up and to be sure the latches were bolted. "If you don't, you run the risk of the animals getting out. Miss Gertrude doesn't take kindly to loose cows and horses. It's something you'd be punished for," Jack said, directing his words to Henry. Henry glanced at Eddy for confirmation, wincing when he nodded in agreement.

....

Meanwhile, in the library, Miss Nellie listed off the daily duties the girls would be responsible for. "In the dorm, you'll need to sweep the rooms, clean the bathrooms, ensure all lamps are topped off with kerosene, and wash the sheets once a week. In addition to the work in the dorm, you'll sweep and dust the classroom and library. Do you have any questions?" The girls, in a bit of a daze, shook their heads. Miss Nellie handed each a cloth and showed them where the brooms were. She had them dusting and sweeping the library in no time. Ruth was surprised at the amount of work to be done. She rolled her eyes.

"This will keep us so busy, there won't be time to eat or sleep," Ruth whispered to Lorene.

7

Clang. Clang. "Let's go feed the dogs," Sammy said. Henry and Sammy left the dorm and went behind the schoolhouse and listened to Miss Gertrude give instructions on how much to feed the dogs.

She walked them to the north side of the building and showed them the location of the dogs' kennels. "Sammy, Jack, and Will, you are responsible for making sure the water trough is clean and has fresh water in it at all times. Without crowding each other, you may feed your dog now. Go to the dining hall when you are done. Do not be late for supper."

The boys and girls chatted about their jobs while they sat at the table waiting for supper. Most complained about how difficult the work would be. Miss Gertrude entered the room, and the children went silent. After supper, Henry and Ruth went to the library to write letters to their father and Kate.

"What are you going to tell them, Ruth?"

"I'm not sure. It's probably a bad idea to write about our jobs. At least for now. I've got a weird feeling about this place."

"I know what you mean. Sammy says things but doesn't explain, so I don't understand what he's talking about."

"Let's write about the walk we took and our new dogs," Ruth said.

"Okay." They scrawled out their letters in silence.

They gave the letters to Miss Gertrude to mail. "You're in luck. Pinehurst is also an official post office. Your parents will receive your letters in a few days," Miss Gertrude said.

....

Henry put out the light and lay down on his cot. *Hoo hoo ho-ho hooowah.* His heart rate quickened. "What's that noise?"

"It's a barred owl. They're harmless. They sometimes make a lot of noise. It'll stop in a minute," Sammy said.

Hoo hoo ho-ho hooowah. A roll of thunder rumbled, vibrating the window as a slight breeze blew the curtains. "I hope it doesn't rain tonight. It gets too hot when the window is shut," Henry whispered.

"It sure was hot today. Let's try to sleep."

"Okay, good night." *Hoo hoo ho-ho hooowah.* Henry covered his head with his pillow. An hour after lights out, Henry tossed and turned. His mind wouldn't stop jumping from one thought to another. He lay on his side and faced the wall. *What was that?* He strained his ears to hear the sound. It was coming from the room next door. *I think that's Alex's room. Is he crying?* He wondered what was wrong. *He probably misses his parents.* A disturbing thought struck him: *Jack said something about punishment around here. I wonder if he got in trouble?* Tired from a long day, his thoughts finally went silent, and he fell asleep.

....

Sunday, August 20, 1905

Pale sunlight shone through the window. Henry, tired from little sleep, rubbed his eyes. "What day is it?"

"It's Sunday, Bible study day in the classroom, and the day before school starts." Sammy rolled his eyes.

"I heard the crying again last night; I think it was Alex. I got to thinking, he's either homesick, or he was in trouble yesterday."

"I doubt if he got in trouble. David probably told him about the punishment Miss Gertrude hands out around here."

"So how bad is it?" Henry asked.

Sammy hesitated. "It depends on what you do to get in trouble. Might be hit with a leather strap on your backside or hit with the strap plus get shut in a tiny, dark closet. It's so small you can't sit down and can barely move around. The closet is saved for the worst troublemakers. A lot more get their backsides tanned than go in it."

"What kinds of things?" Henry bit his lip, his gaze fixed on Sammy.

"Lying to Miss Gertrude or Miss Fannie. They won't put up with it, so don't ever lie to 'em. Hurting any animal, too. Cheating in the classroom is a big one. And being late to class and meals, too. Those are only some of the rules. As long as you behave and follow them, you'll be okay."

"But I don't know what the rest of the rules are!"

"You will. It's part of what Miss Gertrude tells us the first week of school. Trust me, you'll know 'em by next Friday."

"Do only the new kids get in trouble?"

Sammy chuckled. "No, the kids who've been here forever are in trouble all the time. Some say Miss Gertrude chooses one kid to pick on all year. They also say she spanks for no reason at all."

Wide-eyed, Henry stared at Sammy. "Why would she do that?"

"To keep kids in line. C'mon, we need to feed our dogs. We can't be late getting to the dining hall."

....

Several children waited their turn to use the scoops. "It'll take us forever to feed our dogs. We'll be late for breakfast! And get punished!" Wiping the sweat from his forehead with the back of his hand, Henry's stomach churned.

"Yeah, we might," Sammy grumbled.

"What are we supposed to do? I don't want to get punished!"

"Neither do I."

"But we'll be late! We should've left the dorm earlier." Henry's voice went up an octave.

"Well, we didn't. We'll either be in trouble for being late, or we get in trouble for not feeding our dogs."

"I don't want to get punished at all!"

"There's a lot of kids out here. I don't know if Miss Gertrude will punish us since she hasn't gone over the rules yet. Try not to be upset."

"How can I not be upset?" Henry paced back and forth.

Miss Gertrude walked out the back door and scowled at the children. "You waited too long to feed your dogs and will be late to breakfast! Tardiness is unacceptable. Many of you will be late; you'll only have a few minutes to eat. You must arrive earlier next time." She walked back into the schoolhouse, slamming the door behind her.

"C'mon, it's almost our turn." Sammy waved Henry over toward the bucket. The boys fed their dogs and headed inside to the dining hall.

....

Henry was grateful for the silence during breakfast; he didn't want to hear any more about the punishment. Staring at his plate, he picked at his French toast. After eating, Henry went out to find Buster. He welcomed the warmth of the sun on his face. There was something about the indoors that made him feel uneasy. Henry put the rope leash around Buster's neck and led him to the front steps of the school building. The puppy, six months old, was clumsy and fell over him while attempting to get in his lap. Henry had a great time with Buster, briefly forgetting about what Sammy had told him. Not sure of the time and not wanting to be late, he took the leash off Buster and went to the dorm to get ready for Bible study.

After reciting the Lord's Prayer, the children and the field hands turned their attention to Miss Gertrude. "Today's lesson comes from 1 Peter, chapter 2, verses 13 and 14, 'Submit yourselves to every ordinance of man for the Lord's sake: whether it be to the king, as supreme. Or unto governors, as unto them that are sent by him for the punishment of evildoers, and for the praise of them that do well.'" Henry didn't miss a word but didn't understand everything she said. The word "punishment" jumped out at him. He looked at Sammy, who nodded his head ever so slightly.

Miss Gertrude talked about how good and bad behaviors are based on choices. She finished her sermon with, "You always have a choice: to do the right thing or to do the wrong thing. It's up to you."

....

After the noon meal, Miss Gertrude had the children work on their jobs with help, as they would be doing them on their own beginning the next morning.

Mr. Dan, dressed in overalls, dusty boots, and a well-worn Stetson hat, showed Sammy, Jack, and Will how to clean the stalls. "Now remember, when you're done with the stalls, you need to hang the tools back on the wall. They can be dangerous if left on the ground. Then you've got to rake the straw and loose debris from the aisle. Dump it in the same manure pile out back. The wheelbarrows go under the hayloft. Any questions?"

"No, sir, Mr. Dan," Will said. Mr. Dan caught Sammy's eye. Sammy shook his head.

"No, sir." Jack brushed a piece of straw off his threadbare shirt. The boys wasted no time and got to work. Finished, Sammy and Will went to the dorm to clean up while Jack searched for Henry and Eddy.

Jack found the boys in the library. Since the cows and horses were not fed until four o'clock, Henry, Eddy, and Jack had a few minutes to chat. Not wanting to believe everything Sammy had told him about the punishment at Pinehurst, Henry asked the boys if they had ever been in trouble. Jack laughed. "Of course. Everybody gets in trouble." Henry shivered and glanced at Eddy. He nodded in agreement.

"Are they really mean here? I got in trouble at home, but nothing like what Sammy said. How bad is it?"

Jack glanced at Eddy. Henry continued to plead, "Is it true? Do they hit you with a strap and put you in a small closet?"

Jack looked at Henry with his intense dark eyes and nodded. "Yeah, it's true. You'll learn what you can and can't do around here. If you don't break any rules, then you'll be okay. But everybody makes some mistakes."

Henry's face went ashen. He whispered, "How often does it happen?"

"It depends. For some, hardly ever or not at all. Others are in trouble once or twice a week."

Henry mopped the sweat on his brow with his sleeve. "But what do the parents think about the punishment? Why don't they do something about it?"

Jack looked at Eddy. "You tell him."

Eddy's expression darkened. "Miss Gertrude will give us a talk; she'll say we're not to say anything to our parents about our jobs or the punishment. If we do, we'll be in even worse trouble. She never says what the trouble is, but I've heard that the kids who do the worst things are locked in the closet all day. And that's only the beginning. I've never known it to happen, but it gets repeated a lot."

Henry's thoughts were swimming in his head. He didn't want to think about what he was hearing. But how could he not? He slid into a chair and stared at his feet, stroking his chin.

"Don't worry about it. Just follow the rules and you'll be okay," Jack said. "Time to go to the barn." Henry and Eddy followed Jack out the door.

The boys walked in silence under a gray, overcast sky heading for the dilapidated building, its roof aging with orange rust. Jack tugged the big door open, its sun-bleached wood boards warped. The dark sky kept the interior of the barn in shadows. "Sure is spooky in here," Henry said. *Bang!* A window shutter slammed shut on one of the stalls, startling him. *Bam!* Frightened, Chance kicked the stall wall. The wind howled through the gaps in the wooden structure.

"The wind is picking up; we may get a storm. C'mon, let's get busy. The grain is over here." Jack opened the bin, filling a scoop almost to the top. "This is how much grain to feed the cows." He dumped it back in the tub. "Make sure you close the lid tight, or the mice will get in." Jack demonstrated how much to give the horses.

Jack showed Henry and Eddy where the feed buckets were and how to pour the grain in without dropping any. He scaled the ladder to the hayloft. "Up here is the hay. Each cow and horse gets a pad like this." Jack showed the boys how much. "Gather the pads of hay and throw them down from the hayloft." He tossed eight pads onto the aisle and descended the ladder in a flash. "You have to open their doors to give the hay to them, just like the water. You can do it at the same time," he said, picking pieces of hay from his black hair.

Following Jack's instructions, the boys got the buckets and filled them halfway. Jack went to Daisy's stall and showed the boys how to open the door and get her to stand back. "There won't be much old water in the trough, so dump it. Add the fresh water and put the hay in the bin. Then leave. Don't try to pet the animals. They're sort of nice, but they are big and strong and can push past you and get out. Don't let them do it. If they don't back up or if they walk toward you, back out of the stall and close the door." Jack showed them how to make sure the stall door was closed and bolted. "And that's it."

After watching again, Henry wasn't quite so nervous. *I can do this.* Jack asked both boys to repeat what to do to make sure they remembered everything. They told Jack the steps, word for word. "Sounds like you're ready to feed and water them. I'll be watching to make sure you do it right." Jack walked back to the big door and sat down.

The two boys finished with Daisy and moved on to Rosie. Henry opened the bolt, and Eddy walked into her stall with his arm out and his palm up. "BACK." Rosie took a step back, and Henry slipped in with the water and hay. The boys hurried out and bolted the door shut.

"How 'bout if you do the watering and the hay, and I tell them to stand back?" Henry offered.

"Okay." This time, with water and hay ready, Eddy released the bolt on Cookie's door.

Walking into the stall, Henry commanded, "BACK." Cookie stepped back. Eddy dumped the old water and replaced it with fresh water, then placed the hay in the bin. They got out and bolted the door. "That was easy." Henry's confidence was building.

The boys went to Jezebel's stall. Eddy opened the door, and Henry went in and held up his arm with his palm out. "BACK," he ordered. Jezebel blinked but did not move. "Go on, get BACK!" Henry ordered again, this time louder. Jezebel took two steps toward him. Screaming, he turned and ran out of the stall. Tripping over the bucket, he splashed water everywhere. Down he went on his hands and knees. Scrambling, Henry got to his feet and ran outside.

In a flash, Jack headed for Jezebel's stall. Eddy, in a bit of shock, didn't bolt the door in time, and Jezebel pushed her way out of the stall, knocking him to the ground. She approached the entrance of the barn.

8

Jack snatched a rope off the wall and faced Jezebel. Walking toward the lumbering cow, he swung the rope in a circular motion. Trying to get her to stop, he yelled, "NO!" Jezebel sauntered down the aisle toward the big outdoors. Jack swung the rope faster and shouted again. She stopped and blinked at Jack, swishing her tail back and forth. Jezebel turned and walked back into her stall. Eddy slammed the door shut and bolted it. He slid down the side of the stall door panting, his heart pounding.

"Whew! That was close," Henry said, walking into the barn, brushing at the mud on his knees.

"Yeah, it was! You almost let Jezebel out!" Jack laid into Henry.

"What are you talking about?" Henry's voice rose.

"You scared her when you screamed and ran out! If you hadn't scared her, she wouldn't have gotten out of her stall. I told you to back out of the stall if she steps forward. Eddy would've seen her move, and then shut the door before she got out."

"But I forgot. Eddy should have closed the door quicker. It's not my fault!"

"You started it by screaming! Do you realize all three of us would've been punished if Jezebel got out?" Jack's voice rose, his face turning red.

"But, but . . ." Henry sniffed, his chin trembling.

"Stop it! We don't have time to argue. We need to make sure the horses are fed and watered. I think Eddy should be the one to have the horses stand back."

"Yeah, okay." Henry grabbed a bucket to go fill with water. The boys finished their job in silence. Sammy walked in when the boys were leaving the barn and noticed Henry's muddy pants. Henry kept walking and didn't say a word.

Jack told Sammy what happened with Jezebel, and how Henry wanted to place the blame on Eddy. "Well, I guess he'll learn soon enough about how things are around here," Sammy said.

....

Henry went to the schoolhouse and searched for Ruth. He found her dusting the shelves in the library. "Whew, this is no fun." She brushed strands of hair out of her face. Henry walked into the room. "How's your job?" Ruth asked. She saw the mud on Henry's pants. "What happened to you?"

"I think the job's okay. It's a little hard, but I'll get used to it." Embarrassed, Henry didn't mention that Jezebel had almost gotten out. "Um, I uh, tripped over a water bucket and fell." Henry hesitated. "I need to talk to you, Ruth."

"What is it? What's wrong?"

He told Ruth what the others had told him about the punishment, and how horrible it was. "I'm scared, Ruth. What are we going to do? We can't tell Father or Kate. We'd be in a lot worse trouble."

"How do you know they are telling the truth? They may be teasing you."

"I don't think so. Sammy told me before Jack and Eddy did. Why would they all say the same thing if it wasn't true?" Henry's legs turned to jelly, and he sat down before they gave out.

"Hm. I don't know; I haven't heard anything about it. Try not to let it bother you. There's no sense in worrying about something that may never happen."

"But it will happen!" His voice quavered. "They said everyone will be in trouble at some time. I don't want to get in trouble!"

Ruth glanced at the old grandfather clock as it chimed five o'clock. "We need to feed the dogs and dress for supper. Come here, Henry," Ruth reached out and gave her brother a hug.

....

Henry had just finished dressing for supper when Sammy walked into the dorm room. "How did it go this afternoon?"

"Okay, I guess."

"That's not what I heard."

"What did you hear?" Henry's eyes narrowed.

"Jezebel almost got out 'cause you screamed and ran out of her stall."

"That's wrong! Eddy didn't bolt the door in time. That's how she almost got out," Henry said, blustering.

"You don't understand, Henry. Things are different here. It's not like home. Miss Gertrude holds us responsible for anything and everything that goes wrong around here. All three of you would've been punished: you for screaming and running, Eddy for not latching the door in time, and Jack 'cause he was in charge of you two. The sooner you learn that, the better."

"It wasn't my fault," Henry whined.

"Okay. Believe what you want. C'mon, time to go," Sammy said. Henry jammed his hands in his pants pockets and scuffed his feet as they walked to the dining hall. He welcomed the quiet supper; Henry didn't want to listen to any more of Sammy's foolishness.

Henry decided to stay in his dorm room after supper and read. He struggled to keep his mind on his book—his thoughts kept flitting back to earlier that afternoon. Frustrated, Henry closed his book and rubbed his eyes. Sammy came into the room, slamming the door behind him. "Want to play some cards?"

"Yeah, sure." They settled on the floor and played until almost time for lights out.

Once in bed, Henry flipped from his side to his back, and to his side again, unable to fall asleep. He couldn't stop thinking about Jack's words: "You almost let Jezebel out." *That just doesn't seem right.* He turned his thoughts to school. The anticipation of class the next day chewed away at him. He squinted to see if Sammy was awake. The regular rhythm of his breathing told him that he was asleep. Henry turned over and faced the wall, willing himself to go to sleep. A restless sleep finally came, only a few hours before wake-up time.

....

Monday, August 21, 1905

"Ugh. First day of school," Sammy said, groaning.

"At least you don't have a job right after breakfast." Henry yawned. The memory of yesterday's fiasco flashed in his mind, and his stomach fluttered. Slow to get out of bed, he made his cot and washed his face.

....

The aroma of freshly baked bread aroused their appetites. "Smells good. Do you know what we're having?" Henry yawned again. Sammy shook his head. Miss Nellie and Miss Minnie brought in the breakfast plates at seven o'clock. The morning meal consisted of buttered grits with biscuits and gravy. Hungry, both boys finished in no time. Walking out of the dining hall, Henry caught up to Eddy. "Are you ready for this?"

"Yeah, I guess so," Eddy said.

"I hope everything goes okay. I don't want anybody to get out." The memory of the day before haunted Henry.

....

The barn door would not yield to Henry's pull. Eddy gave it a try and inched it open. "That was hard. I'm tired already," Eddy huffed, wiping the sweat off his face. The horses began to whinny and paw at the ground in their stalls, and the cows lowed. "Gosh, they sure are noisy! They must be hungry. Let's hurry up."

Henry opened the horses' grain bin and inhaled deeply. "Their food smells good—kinda like dessert. Have you ever tasted it?"

"Yeah, it has molasses in it. That's what makes it sweet. Try a piece."

Henry popped a kernel in his mouth. "Hm. Not too bad. I think I'd still rather have bacon and eggs for breakfast!"

They gave each animal grain without any trouble. The water and hay were next. Nervous, Eddy opened Daisy's door. "BACK," he commanded, putting his arm out with his palm up. Daisy took two steps back. Henry tossed the hay in the bin and got the water bucket. He replaced the old water with fresh water. They scrambled out of the stall. They bolted the door and checked it twice. "Jezebel is next." Henry's heart fluttered. "Let's be extra careful with her. If you tell her 'back' extra loud, she might not try to come out."

"Yeah, okay." Eddy went into the stall and demanded Jezebel back up. She obeyed and offered no resistance. Next they fed and watered the horses. Henry and Eddy were elated—they were done, and proud they had finished their job without any trouble. The two made sure everything was in its place for the next time and walked toward the bright light which poured into the barn. Eddy gripped the door to shut it when two voices called out to keep it open. Frances and Elizabeth hurried to the barn.

Frances said, "We're here to milk the cows. I'm Frances, and this is Elizabeth."

"Hi. I'm Eddy, and this is Henry. First time here, huh?"

"Yes," Frances answered.

"I was here last year, but this is Henry's first year. So you know how to milk cows?"

"Yes. My grandmother has a farm, and I milk her cow when we visit her. It's an easy job, but I don't know if I'll like milking them every day," Frances said, putting a red ringlet of hair behind her ear.

"I know what you mean," Henry said. "Did the person showing you how to do your work tell you about the latches, and to make sure you bolt them when you are done?"

"Yes. Margaret, who was here last year, also told us Miss Gertrude gets mad if an animal gets out."

"We better get busy milking. See you boys around," Elizabeth said.

....

At a quarter before ten, the bell tolled twice to signal the start of class in fifteen minutes. Sammy and Henry left the dorm and headed to the schoolhouse. When they entered the classroom, Miss Fannie said, "Good morning, boys. Your seats are toward the back of the room. Sammy, you are in the next to the last row all the way on the left. Henry, you too are in the same row, next to Sammy." The other students came in and were directed to find their desks. The youngest sat in the front, and the older children behind them. Ruth, Lorene, Jack, and Will were in the last row.

Miss Fannie introduced herself again and told the students how the learning would take place, with the older children helping the younger students. She then had them introduce themselves. Beginning with the oldest, each child went to the front of the classroom. The students gave their names, where they were from, and what they enjoyed doing.

When the last child finished, Miss Gertrude came in. "We will now talk about making choices and the consequences of your choices. When it comes to any situation, you have a choice to make. You can do the right thing and be praised and rewarded for it, or you can do the wrong thing and pay the consequences. We have rules here at Pinehurst. They must be followed. If you choose to break a rule, you will be disciplined. The type of discipline you receive is based on the violation. For small things, you may be sent to your dorm room for two hours. For some offenses, you will be struck on your backside or the back of your legs with a leather strap." She caressed the strap that was draped around her neck. "For the most serious transgressions, you will be placed in a small closet. This will give you time to think about what you did."

9

There was a collective gasp among the new students. Henry clenched his jaw, sweat popping out on his forehead. *I knew it! They were telling the truth!* He turned around and looked at Ruth. Sliding down in her seat, her eyes were fixed on Miss Gertrude. Ruth chewed at her fingernails, shaking her head in disbelief. Henry turned and faced the front of the room to find Miss Gertrude staring at him. He shivered.

Miss Gertrude continued, "What we do here at Pinehurst is private in nature, meaning you are not to tell your parents about your job or the discipline policy. If you do tell, you will be dealt with severely, and you will need to leave Pinehurst. This is something I know would upset your parents, and you do not want to trouble them. Are there any questions?"

No one raised a hand. Henry scanned his surroundings. Alex was pale, his legs shaking. A few had tears streaming down their cheeks. The old-timers listened with expressionless faces. Miss Gertrude took this time to have them stand and stretch. She talked them through a short exercise routine to help them calm down and be able to focus on the rules.

Miss Gertrude placed a chart on an easel and referred to it as she spoke. "Now for the rules." She used her wooden pointer to draw attention to each numbered line.

"Number eight: No activities or games that are not part of the school curriculum. Number seven: Treat others as you would expect to be treated. Number six: Follow all instructions. Number five: Be on time. This includes school, jobs, Bible study, meals, and lights out at nine o'clock. Number four: No mistreating animals, including letting them loose. Number three: No cheating in the classroom. Number two: No lying to Miss Fannie or to me, or any adult here at Pinehurst. And most importantly, Rule Number One. You are not to tell your parents about the work we do here, or the punishment policy. Do you understand?"

Only the old-timers nodded in comprehension. Henry's eyes glassed over as he stared at Miss Gertrude. He squeezed his eyes shut and mentally shook his head. He looked around; many of the children were staring at her with blank eyes. Miss Gertrude knew she would have to go over the discipline policy and rules several times for them to sink in. The bell rang two times, indicating it was almost dinnertime. Miss Gertrude left the students in Miss Fannie's care.

They walked to the dining hall without a sound. Miss Nellie and Miss Minnie brought out cheese sandwiches and a pear for each child. Miss Gertrude came in, took her seat, and gave a word of thanks. They kept their eyes on their plates while they ate in silence. The students returned to class without saying a word.

"Now that we are back in the classroom, let's talk about the way we learn here at Pinehurst. I introduce the lessons and have the older students begin on their assignments. While they are working, I work with the younger students on the same type of lesson. To reinforce what you've learned, the older students will pair up with a younger child and review the new skill. This way everyone learns, no matter his or her ability. Are there any questions?"

Frances raised a trembling hand. "Yes, Frances, what is it?"

"What will we be learning?"

"Excellent question. Each morning is spent on reading, writing, penmanship, and grammar. When we return from the noon meal, we study arithmetic. After a short break, we study science, history, or geography, depending on the day of the week. Any other questions?" No one raised a hand. "Very well. Let's take a few minutes and go outside."

Miss Fannie took the students to the south side of the school. Behind a wall of trees, they found an oasis in a desert of gloom. Wooden swings hung from the thick branches of stately laurel oaks. Three picnic tables sat under the shade of an enormous southern live oak. Nearby was a cart with jump ropes and balls. The children sprinted to the swings and cart. Ruth and Lorene sat at one of the picnic tables and were joined by Grace and Frances. A gentle breeze helped to cool the warm, humid air. "Sure is nice out here," Frances commented.

"Yes, who would've thought they'd have something like this here," added Ruth.

"So what about your jobs? Which one did you get? I have to milk cows twice a day. It's not easy, and it's no fun," Frances said, her lips curving downward.

"Ruth, Mary, and I are doing housekeeping duties. It's a lot more work than we thought. We won't have much free time at all," Lorene said, rolling her eyes.

"My job is to take care of the chickens. Ruby and me have to feed and water them and gather the eggs. It's a really stinky job." Grace scrunched up her nose. Ruth, Lorene, and Frances chatted, talking about the rules and the punishment, and how they missed their parents and longed for home. Grace sat quietly, listening to the others.

"Grace, what about you? How often will your parents come to visit?" Ruth said.

"I don't have any parents."

"What do you mean?" Frances asked.

"My mother died nine years ago, when I was a baby. I don't know about my father. I was sent to a place for orphans, then here three years ago."

"Oh, Grace! I'm so sorry. How sad." Ruth put her arm around Grace's shoulder.

Grace brushed her golden-brown hair behind her ears and said, "It's okay, I'm used to it. Not having visitors on Sundays used to bother me when I first got here, but it's okay now." She gave a weak smile.

Henry, concerned about Alex, went up to him and asked how he was. "Okay, but I'm still scared," Alex said.

"Just remember what Miss Gertrude told us and be careful not to make any mistakes if you can help it. I think you'll be fine. You seem like a nice boy."

"Thanks, Henry. Can we be friends? I don't have any yet. My roommate, David, and I don't get along."

"Of course I'll be your friend. C'mon, let's get a ball and play catch!"

The children's respite lasted only a short time. Miss Fannie blew a whistle, and they returned to the classroom. Once in their seats, Miss Fannie talked about how everyone would need a book to read at all times. She sent children up to the dorm to collect their library books. Those who didn't have one followed her to the library. Once everyone returned to the classroom, Miss Fannie instructed them to begin reading. Time crept by. Rules and punishments echoed in their thoughts, making reading a chore. The bell rang three times indicating the end of the school day, to the relief of the students. Pleased they had made it through the first day of school, they were happy to leave the classroom.

....

Prior to dismissing the children from supper, Miss Gertrude told Ruth, Henry, and three others to stay behind. Squirming, they thought they had done something wrong and were in trouble. Henry chewed his lower lip. Once the others left the dining hall, Miss Gertrude handed each child a letter.

"Henry! Letters from Father and Kate!"

"You may go to the library to read them," Miss Gertrude said.

Rushing into the room, they ripped open the envelopes. Henry read as he walked, almost stumbling over a chair. He glanced up long enough to sit down, his face breaking into a grin, devouring each word. The letter was about Herman and Kate's trip home, how the house didn't feel the same, and how much they missed him and Ruth. A tear slithered down his cheek.

"It seems like they haven't received ours yet. They didn't say anything about our walk or the dogs." Ruth's eyes scanned the letter.

"They might get them today." Henry said good night to Ruth and walked back to the dorm with a light step. It sure was nice getting the letter from Father. He felt better than he had in days. Exhausted from the stressful day, Henry fell asleep as soon as the light went out.

....

Thursday, August 24, 1905

The children awoke to a gray, wet day. Jogging to the barn, the rain pelted Henry. The massive door was still shut: Eddy had not arrived.

He tugged and pulled on the door, inching it open. He stopped for a moment, taking a break out of frustration. There was still no sign of Eddy. With one last tug, he was able to open the door just enough to slip through. Wasting no time, Henry scaled the ladder to the hayloft and threw down eight pads of hay. He went out to fill the water buckets. *Where is Eddy?*

Eddy ran into the barn. "You in here?" he called out, shaking the rain from his hair.

"Here I am." Henry came in, sloshing water as he walked. "Where were you? There's not much time. Let's get going!"

"Sorry I'm late. One of the new kids stopped me and asked all kinds of questions. I got here as quick as I could."

"Don't just stand there, let's feed them!"

Five minutes later, Emma and Frances squeezed through the door. "You're not done yet?" Frances's voice wavered, her cheeks turning pink.

"No. We got a late start." Henry continued working. "We'll finish with the cows first so you can milk them. You'll need to hurry, so you're not tardy to class."

"Well, you need to be quick!" Emma said.

The boys worked together and finished with a few minutes to spare. They hustled back to the dorm to clean up and change. Reaching the dormitory door, Eddy stopped. "I'm going back to help the girls shut the barn door."

"You'll be late to class! You can't do that."

"It was my fault for being late. I need to help 'em, or they'll be tardy."

The bell rang twice. Henry raced up the stairs to the bathroom to wash up. He scooted to his room, opening the door as Sammy was about to leave. "You're not ready? You better make it snappy," Sammy scolded him.

"I know, I know. I'll be there in a minute." He changed his clothes in a flash and sprinted down the stairs. Opening the door, Emma and Frances rushed in to clean up. "Where's Eddy?"

Reaching the top of the stairs, Emma called out, "He's shutting the barn door. I think he's having trouble with it." Henry let the door slam behind him as he jogged to the schoolhouse. Halfway there he stopped. He was torn between wanting to help his friend and the fear of being punished for being late. Henry looked in the direction of the barn. He hesitated and headed for the schoolhouse.

At ten o'clock Emma and Frances hurried into the classroom, making it to their desks as Miss Fannie opened the door at the front of the room. Eddy's seat was empty.

Miss Fannie's eyes scanned the classroom. "Does anyone know where Eddy is?" A frown crossed her face. Frances looked around the classroom before raising her hand.

"Yes, Frances? Where is he?"

"Emma and I finished milking the cows, and Eddy offered to close the door for us since it's so big and heavy." Henry squirmed.

"I see." Miss Fannie's shoulders dropped. She walked to Miss Gertrude's office and knocked on the door. Walking in, she closed the door behind her. The students heard the muffled voices of the two women. Chewing her fingernails, Ruth eyed the office door. Both women walked out of the office, and Miss Gertrude left the classroom. The students' gaze followed her out the door.

Miss Fannie got the students' attention and introduced the day's lesson. "This morning we will learn about nouns and pronouns." She wrote two sentences on the blackboard.

The back door slammed, startling the children. The seasoned teacher grimaced, knowing what was coming next. Miss Fannie tapped her pointer on the sentences, reading them aloud. She continued, but they listened not to her, but to the heavy footsteps in the hall and the opening of the library doors.

....

Miss Gertrude opened the curtains in the dim library and crossed her arms. "So, Eddy, I have the impression you don't understand the rule about being tardy to class. Is there anything you want to say?" Eddy eyed the leather strap around her neck.

"Y-Yes, ma'am. I went back to the barn to help Emma and Frances close the door since it's so h-heavy."

"It's noble you want to help others, but did you break a rule?" Miss Gertrude slipped the strap from her neck.

"Yes, ma'am." Eddy flinched each time she tapped the folded, well-worn strap on her palm.

"Well, then, you need to be punished."

10

Unable to focus on what Miss Fannie was saying, the students listened to the murmur of voices coming from across the hall. Then silence. A moment later, Eddy howled with each strike of the strap. More silence. Miss Fannie took a deep breath and closed her eyes.

Miss Gertrude paraded Eddy into the classroom and motioned him to his seat, his red eyes staring ahead, oblivious to all. With her lip twitching, Miss Gertrude watched him go to his seat, her head held high. With her fists on her hips, she glowered at the rest of the students before leaving. Miss Fannie continued with the lesson. Unable to pay attention to what she was saying, Henry felt numb. Time dragged by, and the children were getting fidgety. *Clang. Clang.* They let out a communal sigh.

....

When school let out, Henry went to the barn and found Jack, Sammy, and Will cleaning the stalls.

"You're here early," Sammy said.

"I can't believe Eddy got in trouble," Henry said.

"Yep. Get used to it. Like I said, it happens a lot here."

"I'll be back later. I'm taking Buster for a walk." At four o'clock, Henry returned to the barn to find Eddy getting grain out of the bins. "Hey, you beat me to the barn."

"Yeah, I just got here."

"Okay. I'll get the hay and the water." The boys worked while the sound of thunder rattled in their ears. "It's too bad you got in trouble when you were trying to help the girls."

"I'm used to it. I knew it was coming—I broke a rule."

....

Saturday, August 26, 1905

Before dismissing the children from breakfast, Miss Gertrude said, "Today you will work on harvesting fruit or peanuts, depending on your age. Those of you with jobs, you will do them first. We'll meet at the back of the schoolhouse in one hour. The bell will ring once, giving you a ten-minute warning."

"I was waiting for her to tell us we'd have to pick crops or plant something." Sammy pursed his lips.

"It's Saturday! We go to school all week, and we have to work on Saturday, too?" Henry kicked the dirt with his foot.

"Yep," Sammy grumbled.

Once everyone was gathered, Miss Gertrude said, "Most of you will be picking pears or apples with Mr. Dan. Jack, Will, Lorene, and Ruth, you will be harvesting peanuts with Mr. John," Grumbles and moans escaped the lips of the children.

"Okay, if you with me, les' go to the shed," Mr. John said, swatting at a fly. The four followed him, scuffing their feet in protest. Mr. John plucked out five garden forks. "We gonna be diggin' peanuts." They followed him beyond the sheds, along the edge of the woods to a field with nondescript plants. "Here's how we do it." Mr. John demonstrated, all the while taking off his hat and waving it in the air to brush the flies away. "When you finished, jus' drop 'em on the ground. We'll get 'em later." He took a rag out of his bib pocket and patted his forehead.

Ruth wiped the sweat off her face and whispered to Lorene, "I'd rather do housekeeping all day than this!" She swatted a buzzing fly away.

"I know. I'm sweating, and we haven't even started," Lorene complained.

Mr. Dan took the other children behind the sheds to the other side of the pasture. He split the children into two groups. "Half y'all will be picking pears, and the other half, apples. You pick 'em the same way. Come over here and watch me." He gripped a pear and showed the children what to do. "Okay, everybody find one and try it." The children gave it a go, most able to do it on the first try. "When you're done picking it, it goes in the wagon, in the baskets. The apple trees are over there." Mr. Dan pointed to them. "Find a spot and get picking."

Two hours in, Henry said, "My arms are killing me!"

"Yeah, mine, too. And we got to do this all day," Sammy griped. By one-thirty, the children were slowing down, the heat wearing on them. They took a quick water break and continued to work until three o'clock. Those who had afternoon jobs got busy, completely sapped of energy.

. . .

Sunday, August 27, 1905

Henry decided to go to the library to kill time. Surprised to see Ruth engrossed in her book, he walked up behind her and pulled her hair. Ruth jumped. "Henry! Don't do that." She couldn't help but smile at her brother. "Today's the day! I can't wait for Father and Kate to get here. It feels like it's been a month since we've seen them."

"I know. I'm excited, too. I wish they could stay longer though. Two hours isn't long enough."

"Good morning. Bow your heads as we recite the Lord's Prayer." She flipped through her Bible. "Today we will talk about doing good versus doing evil." Miss Gertrude read aloud from 1 Peter chapter 3, verse 17. "Many of you will visit with your parents today for the first time since arriving at Pinehurst." Faces erupted with smiles. "I want to remind you it is God's will to do the right thing and it is evil to do the wrong thing. This includes following all the rules, especially rule number one on privacy. Be mindful of this, or you will suffer from doing evil."

Henry felt a knot growing in his stomach. He glanced over his shoulder at Ruth. She gave her head a slight shake.

Miss Gertrude continued, making an appeal to God for good conscience. When she was finished, Miss Fannie played "Amazing Grace"[1] on the piano.

....

Both Henry and Sammy lay on their cots reading. Henry didn't feel like talking. He wanted to escape to the land of King Arthur. *Clang. Clang.* "Dinnertime. Let's go," Sammy said. They left the dorm and headed to the dining hall. "So, your parents are coming today. That's great. I wish mine were."

"Why aren't they coming to visit? I thought everybody's parents would be here today."

"Not mine." He shuffled along the path. "They only come once a month."

"That's too bad. What are you going to do this afternoon?"

"I don't know. Might ask Jack if he wants to play cards or take our dogs for a walk in the woods."

"You mean Jack's parents aren't coming either?"

Sammy stopped walking. "You don't know? Jack doesn't have any parents. His mother died when he was born, and his father died when he was two years old. He got put in an orphanage."

"How terrible!" Henry opened the door at the back of the schoolhouse, and the aroma of baked ham filled the air. The room was abuzz with whispering. Henry observed the others' faces. It was apparent to him whose parents weren't coming today. Miss Nellie and Miss Minnie came in and handed out the lunch plates. Hungry, Henry finished his meal in no time.

After dinner, children waited on the front porch of the schoolhouse for their parents to arrive. Eddy and David sat on the porch leaning against the building, staring at the end of the drive. Fidgeting, Henry looked at Alex. Alex beamed, bouncing on his toes. Ruth and Lorene sat on the steps giggling, their bright eyes scanning the circular drive. Their gaze settled on the wagon turning off the main road onto the driveway. Mr. John was singing part of the chorus of "Old Folks at

---

1. John Newton, "Amazing Grace," 1779.

Home:"[2] "All de worl' is sad an' dreary ev'where I roam . . ."; his voice trailed off as he drove closer to the building.

Mr. John pulled Ajax and Apollo to a stop in front of the picket fence. Some of the children were squealing with joy and pointing to the grown-ups seated in the wagon. Eddy grinned at David and pulled him up. Mr. John helped the passengers down as children rushed the adults. Henry's heart dropped. Where is Father? He said he would be here today! He looked over at Ruth with a trembling chin. She jumped up and walked over to him.

"It's okay, they'll be here. Father said they were coming." Ruth's voice wavered. The sight of an old buckboard got their attention. The wagon bounced onto the circular drive and drove toward the school. Children strained their eyes trying to identify the occupants. It pulled off the side of the drive and rolled to a stop. Two men exited the wagon then helped the women down, to the cheers of a couple of children. Alex got up and galloped to the wagon. He jumped into his mother's arms, tears of joy rolling down his cheeks.

"They are coming," Ruth said, her voice cracking.

"I hope you're right." Henry kicked at the sand. He watched a small carriage travel up the driveway. The sun shone in Henry's eyes, and it was impossible to make out the driver and passenger. The carriage pulled up on the far side of the buckboard, and the horse shook his head and snorted, rattling his harness. The driver put on the brake and exited the vehicle. A tall man smoothed out his suit coat and surveyed his surroundings.

"Father!" Henry called out. He and Ruth sprinted out to greet him. Charging toward him at full speed, Henry plowed into Herman, almost knocking him over. His arms flung around his father, squeezing him hard. The tension flowed out of Henry's body.

"My goodness, I'm so glad to see you, son." Henry's grip stayed strong, and it took Herman a moment to peel him off. He held Henry at arm's length and gazed into his eyes. "It's okay, I'm here now." Herman embraced him again, then Ruth slid in to get her hug. "Hi, Ruthie, it's great to see you."

"Hi, Father. At first, we didn't think you were coming—you weren't with Mr. John. We were a little scared."

2. Stephen Foster, "Old Folks at Home," 1851.

"I'm sorry, I should've told you in my last letter I'll be using a carriage to come down here."

"I'm glad you're here." Ruth smiled, her eyes glittering as she blinked away tears. "What's the horse's name?" Ruth asked, stroking his forehead.

"His name is Hercules." Herman patted the big chestnut gelding on his neck.

"He sure is pretty." She ran her hand through his flaxen mane.

Herman helped Kate from the carriage. Walking to the children, she smiled. Ruth ran up to Kate and gave her a big hug. "I'm so happy you're here!"

"I've missed you, Ruth. I've looked forward to today for the last week," Kate said, exposing a rare smile. "You'll have to show us around and tell us what all you do here." Kate turned to Henry. "I've missed you too, Henry."

A table was set up in the library with lemonade and snacks for the children and their parents. Ruth explained how the room was full of great books, and they were required to have one to read at all times. "Well, I'm glad to hear it. It was almost impossible to get you to read at home." Herman winked at Henry.

"I found a book I like. It's about King Arthur and his knights."

"I'm glad you're enjoying it."

"Hello, sir. I'm Daniel Bingham, and this is my wife, Laura. We're Eddy's and David's parents," the stout gentleman said. Shy, David stood behind his mother. Eddy was right up front, ready to meet Henry's parents. "Come on boys, say hello."

David mumbled a simple, "Hi."

"Hi, there! I'm Eddy. Me and Henry are friends."

"Hello, Mr. Bingham, Mrs. Bingham. Nice to meet you. I'm Herman Conrader, and this is my wife, Kate. Henry and Ruth belong to us." Herman smiled. "Hello, Eddy. I'm glad you and Henry are friends. Hi, David, nice to meet you, too."

Alex, seeing Henry in the library, pulled his mother into the room. "Mother, there is Henry, the nice boy I was telling you about." The adults introduced themselves and chatted for a few minutes.

Herman, Kate, and the children walked across the entry hall to the classroom. Ruth and Henry told them about the types of things they were learning. Henry mentioned how the older kids helped the younger ones, and how much he liked it. "Oh, and there's a great play area on the side of the school. It's really nice," Henry said.

Miss Fannie walked into the classroom. "Hello, I'm Miss Fannie Anhorn, the teacher. You must be Mr. and Mrs. Conrader. So nice to meet you."

"Yes, Miss Anhorn, pleasure to meet you." Herman shook her hand. "It appears you have an exceptional school here. I hear positive things about it." Herman winked at Ruth and Henry.

"Please, call me Miss Fannie. Thank you, Mr. Conrader. We do try our best."

"Well, it shows."

"C'mon, Father, we've got other things to see!" Henry pulled on his father's arm.

"Okay." He turned back to the teacher and said, "It was nice meeting you. I hope to visit with you again."

"I look forward to it, Mr. Conrader."

Henry and Ruth took Herman and Kate out the back door of the schoolhouse and showed them the garden. They explained how they would be getting the soil ready for planting. "We should do it next week. Then we'll plant our own seeds and watch them grow," Ruth said.

The four walked to the south side of the building to the swings and picnic tables. Henry dashed to the cart and plucked out a ball. "Let's play catch, Father!"

"Sure. Give me your best pitch."

Henry and Herman enjoyed a game of catch while Kate and Ruth sat at one of the shaded picnic tables. "So, Ruth, how are you two doing?" Kate said.

"We're okay. It was hard the first few days. Henry cried a lot. I did too. This place is so different from home. It's been kind of a shock."

"It seems you two have adapted well, though."

"We're trying." Ruth's voice was almost drowned out by barking dogs.

"My goodness, what's all the racket?"

"Oh, those are our dogs! Remember we told you about them in our letters?" Sounding like a fox hunt, the dogs came thundering into the play area barking wildly. "Henry! Find Buster," Ruth called out.

Henry dropped the ball as the pack of dogs sprinted into the play area. "Buster, come here, boy." He grabbed at the dog as he ran by and fell over when Buster bumped into him. "Come here, you!" Henry got the dog to calm down and introduced the clumsy puppy to his father and Kate.

"Well, look at you two! You're made for each other." Herman winked.

Ruth called out Bella's name, and she trotted over to her and sat down. "This is Bella; she's really sweet."

"Yes, she is." Kate leaned down to pet the dog.

"We've got a little while before visiting time is up. Do you want to show us anything else?" Herman asked.

Turning to Henry, Ruth said, "Let's take them on the same walk Sammy took us on the other day."

The four walked behind the schoolhouse and dormitory toward the barn. Expecting to go into the barn, Kate voiced her fear of big animals. "Don't worry, we're not going in the barn. We're headed to the woods!" Ruth said.

"The woods! I think I'd rather go to the barn!"

....

The sunlight filtering through the trees cast shadows among the path and underbrush. The grand pines provided relief from the hot sun. Henry showed Herman and Kate the gopher tortoise burrows. "Let's see if one is in its burrow." He dropped to his knees and peered into the hole. "There's one in there! See it?" Ruth dropped down next to her brother.

"Wow, he's big!" Ruth said. Standing, she brushed off her hands and knees. "Look at it!"

"We'll take your word for it," Herman chuckled.

"It's the first time I've seen one up close!" A smile stretched across Henry's face.

Herman checked his watch, "Hm. We need to start heading back."

Henry's smile disappeared. "Yes, sir."

They arrived back at the schoolhouse to see the other parents preparing to leave. Herman and Kate gave the children hugs and told Henry and Ruth how proud of them they were. Henry, feeling the reality of Pinehurst said, "Father, they, they . . ."

"They what, Henry?" Herman asked. Ruth shot a look at her brother.

Seeing Ruth's expression, his thoughts flashed to Miss Gertrude and Rule Number One. "Um, they, uh, have good food here."

"Glad to hear it. It's time for us to head out. We'll see you again in two weeks, okay?" Herman gazed into Henry's eyes. Henry nodded and hugged his father. "Goodbye, Ruthie." Herman gave her a hug. "We'll miss you two."

"Bye, Father. Bye, Kate." Ruth's voice trembled.

"Bye." Henry waved, swallowing the lump in his throat.

....

The horse snorted and nodded, chewing on the bit as a cloud of dust followed them back to the main road. "Henry acted a bit strange when he said they had good food here," Herman said, turning to Kate.

"Yes, he did. I doubt if it's anything to worry about. He may have said that to keep from crying—I bet he used it as a distraction."

"I hope you're right." He gazed off into the distance, his thoughts questioning Henry's behavior.

....

Henry wiped a tear from his eye, "It sure was nice to see them, huh, Ruth?"

"Yes. I didn't realize how much I missed them until now." Ruth dropped her chin and made designs in the sand with her foot. She stopped and stared at her brother. "What were you going to say to Father and Kate when you said, 'They have good food here?' You were going to tell them about the punishment and the hard work, weren't you?" Ruth waited for Henry to answer. "Henry! Look at me! You can't tell them. We've already seen what happens for being late. The punishment for telling our parents what goes on here is a lot worse."

Henry gazed at Ruth with empty eyes. "I don't want to be here."

"I know. I don't either. But you can't tell Father anything about this place. Miss Gertrude will find out and punish us. At least we get to visit with Father and Kate every other week. Some kids only see their parents once a month, or even less often."

"Sammy told me Jack doesn't have any parents, so nobody comes to visit him. Both his father and mother died when he was real little. He's an orphan."

"Grace is an orphan, too. That's got to be hard on kids, not having parents. I can't imagine being without Father." Ruth wiped away a tear.

"Yeah, I know," Henry said with a catch in his voice. "I know Sammy was upset that his parents didn't visit today. I think I'll try to cheer him up."

11

Henry found Sammy in the dorm playing cards by himself. "What game is that?" Henry asked, watching him move a few cards.

"It's called solitaire." Sammy smirked. "You know, like solitary—being alone."

"Oh, okay. Sorry you didn't see your parents today. Only a couple more weeks before you do, though. That's not too long."

"I know. I miss them. Miss being home. I don't know why my parents even sent me here. I was doing fine at my old school."

"I feel the same way, too. I think it's because my stepmother doesn't like me. I always got in trouble at home; I could never do anything right. It was never like that when my mother was alive."

"What do you mean?"

"I've always done the same things, but I never got in big trouble with my mother. Everything I do makes Kate mad. I don't do things on purpose to make her upset, but she gets mad anyway. It doesn't seem fair."

"She's mad for no reason?"

"Well, no. I do things, and stuff happens. But it's not my fault. She picks on me."

"Okay, I get it," Sammy scoffed and picked up a few cards.

"What? What was that for?"

"Nothin', Henry. It's just been a tough day for me." Sammy went back to his card game.

"I'm going to play with Buster." He changed into his work clothes. "See you later," Henry mumbled, opening the door. Sammy grunted in return.

....

The dogs were still hanging around the schoolhouse, making it easy to find Buster. Henry slipped the makeshift leash around his neck. "C'mon, boy. Let's go." He took the puppy into the pine woods. A slight breeze rustled the silvery, light-green fronds of the palmettos, making the heat tolerable. "Let's go find the tortoises, Buster." He found the spot where he had seen them earlier. To his surprise, one of the tortoises was out and on the path. Henry stopped short. Buster took an attack stance and barked, shattering the silence. "Shh, Buster. Hush!" The dog broke loose and went after the tortoise. On the defense, the tortoise pulled his legs and head into its shell. Buster tried his best to put his mouth on the creature. His teeth left scratch marks on its shell before Henry got control of him. "Buster! C'mon!" He pulled on the leash until Buster complied. They jogged out of the woods and up to the schoolhouse. He saw Eddy heading for the barn. "Wait up!"

Eddy stopped and turned around, "Where have you been? I was beginning to think you forgot about feeding time."

"I was out in the woods with Buster," Henry told him about Buster and the tortoise.

"You need to be careful. Remember the rule about hurting animals? If your dog had hurt him, you would be in trouble."

"I didn't do anything—it was Buster!"

"According to Miss Gertrude you are responsible for him."

Henry frowned. "Okay, okay."

Clang. Clang. Hungry, Henry was glad it was suppertime. He was the second person to arrive in the dining hall and was surprised to see Sammy. "Where were you?"

"I was in the library, reading." Sammy gave a half-hearted shrug. Within minutes, the room was filled with children. Famished, Henry wasted no time in eating his entire supper. Afterward, he followed Ruth to the library.

"What did you do after Father and Kate left?" Ruth said.

"I took Buster in the woods to check if the tortoises were out of their burrows. One was on the path! Are you still reading the same book?"

"Yes, I'm almost done. I'll need to choose another one in a day or two. How about you? Are you still reading about King Arthur?"

"Yeah. With all we do around here, it doesn't seem like there's enough time to read." He told Ruth good night and gave her a hug.

....

Sammy sat on his cot reading, engrossed in his book. He didn't notice Henry come in. "Hi, Sammy."

Sammy put his book down. "Hi."

"Hey, can we play cards? The game you showed me the other day was fun."

"Are you sure? It's against the rules, you know." He giggled. "We might get caught and be whipped!" Sammy gaped at Henry.

"Yeah, I'm sure." The boys played until the bell rang once. "I guess we better stop and get ready for bed."

"Yeah, we should. But how about one more hand?" Sammy tempted.

"Okay, but let's hurry."

The boys finished their game and got ready for bed. *Clang. Clang. Clang.* "Nine o'clock. Hurry up and get in bed!" Sammy said. Henry dove into bed and extinguished the lamp. That night, he was tormented by restless sleep and nightmares.

....

Monday, August 28, 1905

After dinner, Miss Fannie explained how they would learn about plants and gardening during science class. "Today we will prepare the garden for planting. Once the ground is ready, we will study the life cycle of plants, beginning with the seed stage." Most liked the idea of hands-on learning. The old-timers knew better; it was more work, plain and simple.

Miss Fannie took them outside to the garden where Mr. John had sectioned it into different size plots the day before. She directed the children to their assigned areas. After explaining what needed to be done, Mr. John handed out hoes and demonstrated how to pull the old vegetable roots out. Henry eyed the size of his plot. To him, it was huge.

The scorching sun drained the children's energy while they worked. Henry wiped his brow, but not before the sweat trickled down into his eyes, stinging them. After an hour, Miss Fannie let them have a drink of water and wash their hands before returning to the classroom. Once inside, Miss Fannie told them they would work on preparing their plots over the next two days. They groaned in response. She continued with telling them what vegetables they would be planting. To the students' relief, the bell rang three times; school was over for the day.

....

Henry got to the barn early. He heard voices coming from inside. He peeked in and spied Sammy and Will playing cards. Henry, watching the boys intently, didn't realize there was someone behind him. A hand reached out and touched his shoulder. He jerked around to find Mr. Dan standing behind him. At six feet, three inches, tall, Mr. Dan towered over Henry. Mr. Dan placed a finger on his lips in a shushing manner. Henry backed off. He heard Mr. Dan say something about cards. Henry shuddered. The boys walked out first, their heads down. He watched Mr. Dan take the boys into the schoolhouse. He knew Sammy and Will would feel the full wrath of Miss Gertrude's wickedness.

Henry slipped into the barn and waited for Eddy to arrive. "Sammy and Will are in trouble."

"How do you know?" Eddy asked.

Henry told him what he had seen. "What kind of punishment do you think they'll get?"

"They'll be hit with the leather strap, three, maybe four times each. The worst part is Miss Gertrude will wait until the rest of us are in the dining hall and then whip 'em."

84

"Why would she do that?" Henry's eyes widened.

"She does it so everyone can hear 'em yell and cry out. It's supposed to make us want to follow the rules. C'mon, let's get to work." The boys continued talking while they worked, losing track of time.

....

One of the boys' benches in the dining hall was half empty. The children glanced at each other to determine who was missing. "Where's Sammy and Will?" Ruth whispered.

Henry mouthed, "They're in trouble."

Miss Gertrude's gravelly voice thundered somewhere in the building. "Sounds like she's in the classroom," Henry whispered to Eddy.

"Wait," Eddy whispered. To the students' dismay, they heard a smack followed by a wail. Then another smack and another wail. This occurred two more times until the wails turned into a howl. The children in the dining hall sat motionless. They heard Miss Gertrude bark orders again, this time to another child. *Smack!* A whimper. *Smack!* A cry. *Smack!* A howl.

A few minutes later, Sammy, Will, and Miss Gertrude entered the dining hall. The boys sat down gingerly. Taking her seat at the head of the table, she eyed each child before giving thanks. The children squirmed; Miss Gertrude got her desired effect.

Henry stole a glance at Sammy's watery eyes. Will's eyes were rimmed in red and bloodshot. He lost his appetite and nibbled at his food.

....

Henry opened the door to his room to find Sammy lying on his cot reading. "Are you okay, Sammy?"

"Yeah." A grin stretched across Sammy's face.

"What? What is it?"

"I got caught playing cards, and she took 'em. She doesn't know I've got another deck!"

"You're going to play again? After you got punished? You're crazy."

"I'm not crazy. I got careless. I won't let her catch me again!"

"Do you want to go to the library? I'm heading there."

"Nah, I think I'll stay here."

"Okay." He got his book and glanced back at Sammy. Rolling his eyes, Henry closed the door.

Henry sat in one of the overstuffed chairs to read. At one time, he had disliked reading. He now relished it. It allowed him to escape. When he read, he was going on adventures with King Arthur and his knights; he left behind the work and the threat of punishment. Henry read until the bell rang. He made his way back to the dorm, the sun dipping from the sky.

....

Thursday, August 31, 1905

Sunlight peeked through the window. Henry yawned. "C'mon Sammy. Let's get ready." He sat up and rubbed his eyes.

"Yeah, okay." Sammy rolled over and sat up.

"Why haven't you ever told your parents about what goes on here?" Henry asked.

"Because the punishment is bad enough. I don't want to be in worse trouble. You don't understand 'cause you ain't been in trouble yet. Miss Gertrude makes it to where you won't want to tell."

"Well, I'm going to write my Father a letter, and tell him what it's really like here. I know he will want us to come home."

"Don't do it. You'd be making a big mistake. She has ways of finding out about stuff. You'll be caught, whipped, and put in the closet. Let's go, we don't have much time."

....

After breakfast, Henry and Eddy headed for the barn. Henry offered to stay behind and put the buckets away and to check the latches one more time. He waited with the barn door open so the girls wouldn't have to struggle with it. Once they came into view, he left for the dorm.

Henry dawdled along the path to the schoolhouse. He was in no hurry to get to class. A scream shattered the silence. At first, he didn't know where it came from or who screamed. He heard it again. Sounds like it came from behind the dorm. Henry bolted for the barn. To his consternation, Daisy walked toward him, Frances close behind. "Stop!" He put his arms out to try and block the lumbering cow. She kept walking. He tried again, "STOP!" Henry waved his arms. She didn't stop. He had no choice but to back off. Mr. Dan jogged up and threw a rope around her neck and walked the cow back toward the barn. Frances sprinted over to Mr. Dan and Daisy.

"I'm sorry, it was an accident! I didn't mean to let her out," Frances blubbered. Mr. Dan got Daisy back in her stall. Henry felt bad for the distraught girl; he knew what was coming. His stomach was tied in knots.

....

The children arrived in the classroom unaware of what was about to happen. The bell rang, and they saw Frances's seat was empty. A sense of uneasiness spread throughout the room.

A cry fractured the silence as Frances yelped out in pain. The children winced. The yelp was followed by a shriek and then wailing. Henry squeezed his eyes shut, a wave of nausea washing over him. He swallowed, trying to push the burning liquid back down. Miss Gertrude and Frances entered the classroom. Shaken, Frances went to her seat. Miss Fannie dropped her head for a moment before continuing with the lesson.

....

Saturday, September 2, 1905

"I can't believe there were four kids punished this week. Does it get any better?" Henry said.

"Not for a while. Miss Gertrude likes to show what happens if kids don't follow the rules. She'll get everybody at some point." Sammy shook his head.

Henry shuddered. "I felt bad for Frances. She made a mistake. It's not like she broke a rule on purpose."

"I've been trying to tell you; it doesn't matter if it's a mistake, or if somebody forgets something. They'll be in trouble."

Miss Fannie and Miss Gertrude entered the dining hall. Surprised to see Miss Fannie, the children took notice. "Good morning. The rain on Tuesday and Wednesday kept you from preparing your garden plot. You did not finish, so we must finish today to keep on schedule. We will meet in the garden at eight-thirty—in one and a half hours." Miss Fannie turned and left the room.

Sammy rolled his eyes. "It's work, work, work. All the time," he whispered to Henry.

....

The children labored under the blazing sun, hoeing rows in the soil. The heat set in, making the work miserable. By eleven o'clock, all had finished. Henry looked at his hands. They were blistered, red, and painful. He trudged to the dorm and went to the bathroom to wash up, the cool water soothing his overworked hands. He went to the dorm to find Sammy lying on his cot, reading. "That sure was hard work! Now I have blisters."

"Yep. Welcome to Pinehurst."

"I wish I were home." Henry's voice cracked.

"Yeah, me, too. Want to play cards?" Sammy cracked a grin.

"Sure."

....

Later that afternoon Henry found Sammy behind the kitchen, brushing Duke. "Hey, Sammy, want to go to the creek? We can take our dogs."

"Yeah, we can go." The boys put the leashes on their dogs and headed out for the creek.

They took their shoes off and rolled up their pant legs. The orangish-brown water was refreshing as they waded in. Henry was delighted that a school of minnows darted in and out of the vegetation near the bank. "Look at the size of that frog!" Henry said. *Plop!* It jumped off a half-rotted tree branch and into the water, disappearing from sight.

The boys and their dogs walked in the shallow water, keeping close to the edge. "A crawdad! You ever ate one?" Sammy said.

"No. How do they taste?" Henry scrunched his face, peering into the dark water.

"They ain't bad. Taste sorta like fish." The boys continued on for a few minutes. "Don't know what time it is, but I know we've been here for a while. I need to go back and clean the stalls. Let's go."

"Sure was fun." The boys and dogs jogged along the trail back to the entrance of the woods. Sammy ran to the barn. Henry played with Buster until it was time to do his job.

"Hi, Eddy." Henry stood and told Buster to go.

"Hi. What've you been doing?"

"Sammy and I went to the creek. We saw a crawdad. You ever seen one?"

"Yeah, we got them back home." The boys headed for the barn. "I can't believe Daisy got out the other day. Poor Frances." Eddy dragged his feet on the sandy path.

"I know. I hope it doesn't happen to us."

"It won't if we're careful." Eddy filled the scoop with grain. They finished and left for the dorm.

Henry got washed up and headed to his room. Sammy was lying on his cot, reading. "Hi Sammy, is there time to play slaps before supper?"

"Nah, we'd barely get started before we'd have to stop. Let's play later."

"Okay." Disappointed, he sat on his cot and picked up his book. Henry flipped through the pages and realized he was almost finished. He would need to find another book soon. He got comfortable and read.

The bell rang and Sammy stood. "Quit reading. We've got to go."

"I'm almost done. I've got a couple of pages left. Go on without me. I'll be there in a minute."

"Okay, but hurry." Sammy walked out the door.

Henry finished the last page and closed the book. *That sure was a great story.* Thinking about the ending, he stood and stretched. *Thunk.* Henry was brought back to reality. The downstairs door! A cry escaped his lips. Dashing out of the dorm room, Henry raced down the stairs and sprinted to the schoolhouse. Once inside, he rushed to the dining hall. When he made it to the doorway, he stopped short. He saw Miss Gertrude standing at the head of the table, her arms folded across her chest, her beady eyes piercing him.

12

"You are late, Henry." A look of satisfaction flashed in the old woman's eyes.

Taking two steps backward, fear gripped Henry like the jaws of a hungry creature, crippling him, holding him captive. He opened his mouth to scream, but no sound escaped his lips.

"Come with me." She walked past him and out the door. "We're going to my office."

"Y-yes, ma'am." Henry gasped for air. *This can't be happening!* With his heart pounding in his ears, he followed Miss Gertrude into her office.

"You were late for supper. You broke a rule. Do you have anything to say for yourself?" Miss Gertrude removed the strap from her neck. Henry's eyes grew wide.

"I'm telling my father!" Henry blurted out. His entire body shook.

She locked eyes with Henry. "Oh, are you now? I dare you. You think getting hit with a strap is bad? Go ahead, Henry. Tell your father." Miss Gertrude's lip curled. "The punishment for being late is three lashes with the strap. Bend over and place your hands on my desk." Henry did as he was told. A sense of lightheadedness took over, and things went gray.

Smack! Henry wailed. *Smack!* Henry howled. *Smack!* Henry bellowed. He fell to his knees, his head spinning. His vision went dark, then black.

····

Miss Gertrude fanned his face and shook him. "Henry, wake up."

"Where am I?" he whispered. Henry searched his surroundings. His eyes flew open wide when he laid eyes on the old woman. The icy fingers of terror seized his being.

"You're in my office. We need to go to the dining hall," Miss Gertrude said. Henry's legs almost gave out as he stood. She steadied him and they walked to the dining hall.

The mood in the dining hall was somber. Ruth picked at her food, weeping. Staring at her plate, she was filled with a despair she had not felt before. Maybe Henry's right; perhaps we should tell Father.

After supper Ruth went to the library. Worried about her brother, she couldn't concentrate on her reading. "Henry! Are you okay?" She jumped up and rushed over to him as he entered the room. Trembling, Henry held on as she comforted him. "It'll be okay. Shh. It's okay." He relaxed a little and loosened his grip. Ruth held him out at arm's length and peered into his eyes. His face flushed; a solitary tear fell from his chin.

"I-It was horrible, Ruth. I told her I would tell Father, and she d-dared me to. She said if I did, the punishment would be even worse than the whipping I g-got," Henry choked.

"We won't tell Father. You won't be in worse trouble."

Sammy spoke up, "Henry, you okay?"

"I guess so." His lips quivered.

"I can't believe you told her you were going to tell your father. I don't think anyone has done that before," Sammy said.

"It just came out. I didn't mean to say it."

"Well, if I were you, I wouldn't tell her again." Sammy chose a book and left the room.

"Did you finish your book? Do you want me to help you find another one?" Ruth asked.

Henry nodded. "That's why I was late. I had a couple of pages to go, and it took longer to read than I thought."

"Let's take a look. Hmm. Well, there's *The Call of the Wild*,[1] *Treasure Island*,[2] *The Wonderful Wizard of Oz*,[3] and *Adventures of Huckleberry Finn*.'[4] There are other ones also."

"What is *Treasure Island* about?"

Ruth flipped through the first few pages and scanned the words. "Buccaneers and buried gold."

"Okay, I'll take it." Henry sniffed, sat down, and opened the book. He flipped through it, reading bits and pieces. "Looks like it will be good. I'm going back to the dorm to read." Henry returned to the dorm, the sky bathed in hues of red and orange as the sun slipped from the sky.

He opened the door to find Sammy reading. Sammy sat up and closed his book. "Find another book?"

"Yeah, *Treasure Island*."

"I've read it. You'll like it." Sammy looked at Henry's expression and said, "What's the matter?"

Henry sat on his cot. "I know I was late to supper, but I was doing something Miss Fannie told me to do."

"Yeah, you were doing what you were told to do. You also broke a rule. Not breaking a rule is more important. It was your own fault for getting into trouble."

"I didn't do it on purpose."

"On purpose or not, you still broke a rule."

"Don't they know people make mistakes?"

"Sure, but it doesn't matter. To them, the rules are everything, especially Miss Gertrude. Once you realize that, you won't get in trouble. It took me a while to learn that. After getting into trouble a few times, I finally got it. Yeah, I got in trouble a few days ago 'cause I

1. Jack London, *The Call of the Wild*, 1903.
2. Robert Louis Stevenson, *Treasure Island*, 1883.
3. Frank L. Baum, *The Wonderful Wizard of Oz*, 1900.
4. Mark Twain, *Adventures of Huckleberry Finn*, 1885.

was playing cards. But it was my fault. I broke a rule, so I got punished. I deserved it."

"Okay. I want to read my book now." The boys lay on their cots, reading. Henry read the first page twice and still didn't comprehend it. He was thinking about what Sammy had said. *I didn't break a rule on purpose.*

....

Sunday, September 3, 1905

"Good morning. Let us pray." The children bowed their heads and prayed. "Today's lesson is on trustworthiness." Miss Gertrude's eyes were fixed on Henry. She opened her Bible; "We will read from Proverbs this morning. Chapter 11, verse 13: 'A talebearer revealeth secrets: but he that is of a faithful spirit concealeth the matter.'" For the next hour, Miss Gertrude expanded on the verse. She interpreted it to mean the importance of keeping silent about the activities at Pinehurst. "You do not want to be a talebearer, for it is evil. I remind those of you whose parents are visiting today to be faithful to God and not share everything about Pinehurst."

Henry went to the dorm, got his book, and went to the library. Sammy and Eddy were sitting at one of the tables, chatting. "Some Bible lesson, huh?" Sammy said, leaning back in his chair.

"Yeah. I know she was talking about me." Henry sat at the table, across from Eddy.

"Are you still thinking about telling your father?" Sammy asked.

"It's the only way out of here," Henry said.

"Are you crazy?" Dumbfounded, Sammy stared at him.

"How else can anybody leave here? It's like we're prisoners. I don't know about you, but I want to go home." Henry's shrill voice was getting louder.

"Shh! We all want to go home. Nobody wants to be here. But telling our parents ain't the way to do it."

"Then how?"

"I don't know, but it ain't worth the punishment. Do you want to risk it?"

"I want out of here!"

"Do what you want." Sammy stood. "Let's go, Eddy."

The boys left the library, leaving Henry alone with his scattered thoughts. *I could tell Father not to say to Miss Gertrude I told him. He could make up some reason to take us out.* The library door opened.

"Hi, Henry. How are you doing? Are you feeling better?" Ruth asked.

"I'm doing okay. I've been thinking. The only way out of here is to tell Father."

"Don't do it! Miss Gertrude will find out. You'll be punished!"

"I'll probably be punished for something anyway. At least I can try. I've got to get out of here. As bad as it was at home with Kate being mad at me all the time, it was nothing like it is here."

"I don't want to be here, either. But telling Father would be a mistake."

"Yeah, Sammy says the same thing." Tired of talking, he opened his book. "I want to read now. What are you going to do?"

"Lorene and I are taking Bella and Tippy for a walk. Please don't tell Father. I don't want you to get into trouble." She put her arm around his shoulder and gave him a gentle squeeze before leaving. Henry moved to one of the overstuffed chairs and got comfortable. Wrapped up in his book, he didn't move until the bell rang for dinner.

....

Henry watched the parents of other children arrive for their visit, and a twinge of disappointment hit him. *I wish Father were here. I'd tell him about the punishment now. Maybe I should write him a letter.* He mulled over his thoughts. Henry decided writing a letter to Herman was the only answer. He went back to the dorm to fetch his paper and pencil. Henry sat at one of the tables, pencil in hand. He stared at the paper. His hand shook as he wrote.

Dear Father and Kate,

How are you? I miss you. I can't wait until you visit again on Sunday. The other day, I took Buster for a walk in the woods. I took a wrong turn and almost got lost! I found my way back, but I was scared for a little while. We're getting our garden plots ready to plant seeds. I will grow tomatoes. It's kind of fun but has been hot. The work in the garden goes with what we are learning in science. Miss Fannie is teaching us about the life cycle of plants. I can't wait until it's time to pick the tomatoes! I started a new book. It is called *Treasure Island*. It is about an old sailor and a treasure chest. It is good. I need to tell you something. Miss Gertrude whips kids who break rules. I was late for supper and I got whipped. It was terrible. I want to come home, Father. I'm scared. I don't want to get whipped again. It hurts. Can you take me and Ruth home when you come on Sunday? Please?

P.S. Please don't tell Miss Gertrude what I told you. We are not allowed to tell our parents about the whippings, or we will get in worse trouble.

Love, Henry

With hands shaking, he folded the paper and placed it in the envelope. Henry sealed it and rubbed his hand over it, making sure it would not open by accident. *I'm glad that's done!*

....

Monday, September 4, 1905

Light rain spattered against the window screen in room number four. "C'mon, get up," Sammy said. Standing, he shut the window. "Glad it's raining. Hopefully we won't have to work in the garden this afternoon."

Henry sat up on his cot yawning. "Ugh. I'm still tired. I wish we didn't have school today."

After breakfast Henry and Eddy walked to the barn. "Do you ever go out in the woods?" Henry asked.

"Yeah, I take Chewy for walks out there sometimes." The boys got the grain and fed the animals.

"We were out there the other day and saw some deer up close. It was special."

"The best time to go is at night."

"At night? How do you see when it's dark?"

Eddy laughed. "During the full moon, silly."

"Aren't you scared to go out there at night? I would be!" He ascended the ladder and threw down the pads of hay.

"Aw, there's nothing to be afraid of. Just bobcats. And panthers. And bears!" Eddy laughed.

"They're out there?" Henry gawked at Eddy.

"Yeah, I'm serious. They live in the woods. I never saw a bear, but I've seen bobcats. Heard panthers too. Want to go?"

"Wouldn't we get in trouble?" Henry darted into Daisy's stall, giving her hay.

"Sure we would. If we got caught." The boys finished up their work with no more discussion of sneaking out into the woods.

....

The rain dissipated and the sun broke through the clouds. At one-thirty Miss Fannie announced they were ready to go to the garden to do their planting. The students groaned. Once outside, Mr. John handed out bags of seeds. After explaining what to do, Mr. John dropped one into the hole and covered it with soil. "Any questions?" No one raised a hand. "Okay, then. You ready t' plant your seeds." Mr. John walked over to where Miss Fannie was standing. He took a grimy handkerchief out of his overalls bib pocket and wiped his face. "Sure is hot ou' here."

Miss Fannie pressed a cloth to her cheeks. "Yes, it is."

"This ain't no science lesson. It's work!" Sammy complained to Jack.

"Yeah, it never ends." Jack frowned. By a quarter to three, everyone was done. Sammy, Will, and Jack headed over to the barn.

Henry and Eddy sat down under the shade of a laurel oak. A slight breeze cooled the boys' sweaty faces. "I've been keeping track of the moon, and it'll be full next week. You want to go, Henry?"

"I don't know. I don't want to get in trouble."

"Oh, c'mon. It'll be fun. We won't stay gone long."

"Who else are you asking?"

"Sammy and Jack. They've done it before. I'll probably ask Will, too." Eddy stood. "Let's head on over to the barn."

....

After supper Henry went to the dorm and got his book and the letter to his father. He decided he wouldn't tell anyone about the letter. He tucked it into his book and went to the library. Eager to escape, he opened his book and began to read. Absorbed in the world of mystery and intrigue, Henry didn't hear the door open.

"Hello, Henry."

Startled by the gravelly voice, he said, "Hi, M-Miss Gertrude."

"It appears you're enjoying your book."

"Um, yes, ma'am." He squirmed.

Miss Gertrude went to the bookshelf and skimmed the titles. She pulled a book off the shelf and leafed through the pages. Closing the book, she placed it back on the shelf. Miss Gertrude scanned the books.

She picked up another book and glanced at the first few pages. Miss Gertrude closed it and put it under her arm. She turned and faced Henry. "Reading is so entertaining, isn't it, Henry?" Miss Gertrude's stare made him squirm.

"Yes, ma'am. I like r-reading." His stomach tightened. He remembered the letter. "Um, Miss Gertrude? I have a letter. Would you please mail it for me?" He took it out of his book and held it out.

She took the letter from him. "I will post it in the morning. Good night, Henry." She turned and walked out the door.

He opened his book and continued where he had left off. He attempted to finish the chapter, but his thoughts drifted to Miss Gertrude. He replayed the encounter with her in his mind. *She sure acted strange.* The bell rang, jolting him from his thoughts. He picked up his book and went to the dorm.

....

"Where were you? I was beginning to wonder about you." Sammy shook the hair out of his eyes.

"I, uh, was in the library reading. Yeah," Henry mumbled.

"Are you okay? You don't sound like it."

He searched his mind for an answer. "I'm tired. It was hard working in the garden today."

"Wasn't much fun. At least the worst of it is over."

Henry changed into his nightshirt and lay down. "Good night."

"Night." Sammy fell asleep, his raspy breathing sounding like a small buzz saw cutting through a log.

Henry was exhausted but couldn't sleep. A lump smoldered in his throat. *Maybe I shouldn't have written it.* But it's the only way out of here! He tossed and turned for hours.

....

Tuesday, September 5, 1905

"Now that we've planted our seeds, we will learn about what all plants need. No matter what kind, they need the same three things. To help introduce the concept, I'd like to draw your attention to the blackboard." After the lesson Miss Fannie said, "Let's go outside for some free time."

Puffy white clouds drifted across the sky, providing some relief from the sun's burning rays. Henry took a ball from the cart and jogged up to Alex. "Hi, want to play catch?"

"Yes!" The boys played until their arms got sore. "Whew, Henry, I'm getting tired. How about you?"

"Yeah, I've had enough for now."

Henry and Alex sat beneath the shade of one of the massive oaks, welcoming the breeze. "Sorry you got in trouble. Was it bad?" Alex asked.

"Yeah. I got in trouble at home, but it was never as bad as it is here."

"I'm scared, Henry. I don't want to get in trouble." Alex blinked rapidly and sniffed.

"You're doing fine. You won't get in trouble because you follow the rules. I broke the rule about being late. That's why I got whipped." In an instant, Henry was hit with the thought, *that's why I got whipped.*

....

Eddy and Henry arrived at the barn early and found Sammy, Jack, and Will still cleaning stalls. "Phew! What a dirty job." Henry pinched his nose and laughed.

"You laugh now. Just wait. If you're here next year, this will be your job." Sammy brushed the sweat off his forehead, leaving a smear of dirt in its place.

"Next week is the full moon. Anybody want to go for a walk in the woods?" Eddy's eyes sparkled.

"Yeah, I'll do it." Sammy didn't hesitate.

"I'll go," Jack said, continuing to work.

Eddy asked Will, "How about you? Want to go?"

"I don't know. Sounds fun and all, but I don't want to get in trouble."

"Okay. Well, you have time to decide. It won't be for another week." Eddy faced Henry and stared him in the eye, smiling.

"What? Why are you looking at me like that?"

"You're going, aren't you?" Eddy raised an eyebrow.

Feeling pressured, Henry squeaked, "Yeah."

13

Thursday, September 7, 1905

Rolling thunder rattled the window in room number four. Henry changed into his work clothes and headed to the barn before the afternoon rain showers made their presence known. Jack, Sammy, and Will were still cleaning the stalls when he slipped through the narrow opening of the door. "Hi," Henry called out.

"Hey, Henry," Sammy grunted, tossing a load of horse droppings into a wheelbarrow. He hung the pitchfork up, grabbed a rake, and raked the aisle, clearing out the debris. "Whew, glad that's done." Sammy wiped the sweat off his face and headed for the door. Jack and Will put the wheelbarrows away and hurried out of the barn to try and beat the rain. Mr. Dan managed to get the cows and horses in the barn before the clouds opened up.

Tap! Tip, tip, tap, tik, tap! Tap, tik, tip, tip, tak, tap! Rain pelted the tin roof. In a few seconds the raindrops turned into the sound of a hundred tap dancers. "Wow, it's coming down hard," Henry said to himself. He walked to the front door and peeked out. Here came Eddy, running at full speed. He darted through the door, barely avoiding a collision with Henry.

Soaking wet, Eddy shook the water from his hair. "I don't think I've ever seen it rain this bad."

Henry peered out the open door. "I know. I can't even see the dorm. C'mon. Let's get started." After a few minutes, the rain abated to a light drizzle. They finished and scooted to the dorm.

....

Henry opened the door to his room to find Sammy reading. "Hey."

"Hi," Sammy said, closing his book. "So, are you going out in the woods during the full moon?"

"I don't know. Sounds kind of risky to me."

"We go about midnight. Miss Gertrude and the other grownups are already in bed asleep by then."

"What's so special about the woods at night?"

"The animals! All kinds come out at night. Ever seen a possum up close? They look like huge rats. There are all kinds of weird sounds, too. Animals calling out to each other, and the frogs! You've never heard so many frogs."

"Sounds like it would be fun, but I don't know."

....

After supper Henry and Ruth went to the dorm and got their books. They returned to the library to find a few children immersed in their reading. Henry opened his book to chapter four and was drawn into the action. He didn't notice Miss Gertrude had entered the room.

"Henry?" Her voice spooked him. He dropped his book.

"Yes, M-Miss Gertrude?" Henry gulped, standing.

She looked him in the eye without blinking. "A letter arrived for you today."

"Thank you." He took the letter from her and sat down.

"It's always nice to receive a letter, isn't it Henry?"

"Um, yes, ma'am."

"Ruth, here's a letter for you as well." Miss Gertrude handed her the envelope. Turning to leave, Miss Gertrude leered at Henry again, her expression fixed in her perpetual frown. Henry and Ruth ripped the envelopes open and read their letters. Ruth smiled and giggled as she read. Henry took his time reading his father's letter. A warm feeling flowed through him.

Ruth said, "She acted strange, don't you think?"

"Uh, yeah, I guess so." He thought about the letter he'd asked her to mail on Monday. *Does she know about it?* A moan escaped his lips.

"What?" asked Ruth.

"Um, nothing." Henry stood. "I'm going back to the dorm now. See you tomorrow."

"Okay." Ruth's gaze followed Henry out the door.

....

Friday, September 8, 1905

Almost finished with the stalls, Jack called out, "Hey, Will, both me and Sammy raked the aisle twice this week. It's your turn to do it."

"I'll do it tomorrow." Will walked out of Daisy's stall.

"No, you'll do it today. It's only fair," Jack spoke in a stern voice.

"You're not the boss!"

Jack dropped the pitchfork and walked out of Daisy's stall and into the aisle. He snatched a rake off the wall and held it out. "Do it! It's your turn, Will."

Will pushed it out of Jack's hand. "Oh yeah? Try and make me," he dared. In a flash, Jack lunged at Will, shoving him to the ground. Will jumped up and shoved him back. Jack went after Will again, this time swinging his fists. A blow landed on Will's arm. He came back and swung his fist, punching Jack in the jaw. Jack fell to the ground. He got up and swung again, aiming for Will's face. *Thwap!* The punch hit its mark. Will staggered backward. Jack went for him a fourth time but stopped short at the sound of heavy footsteps.

"Boys! Stop!" Mr. Dan's voice thundered. He seized Jack by his shirt collar and flung him away from Will, sending him sprawling to the ground. "You kids know you ain't supposed to fight! Stand up, boy." Mr. Dan snatched Jack up by the collar. "You two are coming with me." He hauled both boys off to Miss Gertrude's office.

"Whew. Glad it wasn't me." Sammy picked up the rake and cleared the aisle.

Eddy and Henry watched Mr. Dan walk Jack and Will to the schoolhouse. "I wonder what they did," Henry said. Eddy shrugged. They walked into the barn.

"Sammy, what happened?" Eddy asked.

"They got in a fight over who's turn it was to rake the aisle. Both Jack and Will won. I'm the one who has to do it. Lucky me. But they'll have to pay for it."

....

Miss Gertrude slipped the strap from around her neck and glared at each boy. "I understand you boys were fighting. Do you boys know what rule you broke?" Her eyes narrowed.

"Uh, yes, ma'am. Treat others as you would want to be treated." Jack stared at the floor.

"Yes, Jack. Since both of you were involved, you both will be punished." When she was done, she led them to the dining hall.

Henry stopped eating and stared at his plate. Sammy nudged him with his elbow. "You need to eat," Sammy mouthed. He acknowledged Sammy by shoving a piece of tasteless potato in his mouth. Henry was relieved when Miss Gertrude stood and dismissed them from the dining hall.

The boys headed for the dormitory and got their books. Finding the library empty, they plopped down on overstuffed chairs. It wasn't long before Henry was wrapped up in his book. Sammy glanced at the clock: quarter to eight. "I think I'm going back to the dorm. You staying here?"

"No, I'll go with you." Henry's thoughts flashed back to the day when Miss Gertrude came into the library while he was reading. *I don't want her to talk to me again.*

The setting sun was blocked by thick, greenish-gray clouds. "I hope we make it before the rain comes," Sammy said, as they left the schoolhouse. Full of rain, the clouds began to weep. The rain came, dribbling at first. The boys got to the dorm when the deluge hit, barely making it inside. Henry opened their door to find the wind whipping the curtains as rain pelted the screen. He slammed the window shut.

"Want to play cards? We have about forty minutes before lights out. Want to play slaps?"

"Sure." The boys were able to play a few hands before the bell rang. Sammy put the cards away, and the boys got cleaned up and ready for bed. Knowing they only had a few minutes, Henry opened his book and began reading. *Clang. Clang. Clang.* At nine o'clock he extinguished the light. That night Henry dreamed he was on a great adventure searching for treasure chests.

....

Saturday, September 9, 1905

After breakfast Miss Gertrude got the children's attention. "Today you will be harvesting vegetables. Mr. John and Mr. Dan will be meeting you behind the schoolhouse in one hour. The bell will ring once as a ten-minute warning."

"Again? We just picked fruit a couple of weeks ago. And we lose another Saturday?" Henry frowned.

At eight-thirty, the children were gathered behind the schoolhouse. "Okay. Half of ya'll be workin' with me. We be pickin' beans and peppers. The rest of you will work with Mr. Dan pickin' squash and pumpkins," Mr. John said.

....

By ten-thirty the sun was beating down on the workers. "Let's stop for a water break," Mr. Dan said. The children were thankful for the respite.

"Whew, my arms are hurting," Ruth said.

"Mine began hurting a while ago," Lorene said, brushing her hair out of her eyes.

"I hope we're not out here all day." Ruth wiped her brow with her forearm.

They broke for lunch at noon. At twelve-thirty the children were back at it. Mr. John was putting in a good bit of effort, since the children were just not able to work fast enough. Two hours later they took another water break. "Sammy, Will, and Jack, you'll have to leave here in thirty minutes to go clean stalls," Mr. Dan said.

"Yes, sir," Sammy said. Smiling, he glanced at Jack. "You know, I'm looking forward to cleaning the stalls!"

"You and me both." Jack chuckled.

At four o'clock Mr. John and Mr. Dan had the children stop. Those who had afternoon jobs got busy. "I don't think I've ever been this tired before," Ruth said, dusting a table in the library.

"You got sunburned. Your face is all red," Lorene said.

"It does hurt a little." Ruth touched her cheek. At five o'clock she stopped. "Sorry, Lorene, but I can't do anymore." Ruth put her dusting cloth away and headed for the dorm. The cool, fresh water felt good on her face and arms. Looking in the mirror, she saw just how sunburned she was.

....

Ruth slid onto a bench next to Frances. "Hi," Ruth said.

"Hi. Rough day today, huh?" Frances asked.

"I'll say. I can't believe how tired I am and how red my face is."

"Are your parents coming tomorrow for a visit?"

"Yes, are yours?" Ruth said.

"Yes. Just be sure to not tell your parents that you got sunburned from working all day yesterday. Miss Gertrude will punish you if you do."

"What do I tell them? Surely they'll notice!"

"You need to make up something. Tell them you were on the playground jumping rope or tossing balls with some of the girls."

"I don't want to fib!"

"You're going to have to; you don't really have a choice. Emma told me it happened to her last year. She told her parents that she had to work. They said something to Miss Gertrude, and she told them that Emma made it up. They believed Miss Gertrude. When Emma's parents left, she got whipped and put in the closet."

Ruth shuddered. "Okay, I'll come up with something to tell them."

....

Sunday, September 10, 1905

"Today I will read from Romans, chapter 13, verses 1 and 2." She read them and said, "Let me put this in words you'll understand. You're the souls who are under the authority of the grownups here at Pinehurst. God is almighty and ruler of all. God has given the adults here the power to make rules and make sure they are followed. If you are against the rules, then you are against God's law. Those of you who choose to break a rule will be faced with eternal punishment from God." Henry winced. "Today we will sing the hymn, 'Come Closer to Me.'[1] Miss Fannie will provide the musical accompaniment on the piano."

When they finished singing, Miss Gertrude said, "I want to leave you with a final thought. You may be tempted to break your silence about the activities here at Pinehurst. Be forewarned: do so and face God's wrath. You are dismissed." Miss Gertrude closed her Bible and walked to her office.

Henry followed Ruth to the library. "What a Bible lesson, huh, Ruth?"

"Yes. It's the same type of sermon every Sunday. She sure doesn't want us to tell our parents about this place."

He felt a tightness growing in his chest. "Yeah, I know."

"I can't wait to see Father and Kate! It seems like it's been forever since they were last here." Ruth smiled. Wrinkling her brow, she said, "They're going to notice my face is red. Frances told me not to say anything about the work we did yesterday. I guess I'll have to fib to them."

"After today's Bible lesson, I can see why."

"What do you think we should do with them today?" Ruth asked. "We didn't show Father and Kate the barn. The cows and horses will

1. Barney E. Warren, "Come Closer to Me," 1900.

be out in the pasture, won't they? So Kate won't need to worry about the animals. We can take Father to the pasture to see them," Ruth said.

"Yeah, okay."

....

After dinner the children whose parents were coming waited on the porch of the schoolhouse. Sammy, who had not seen his parents since arriving at Pinehurst, was excited. "I'm glad your parents are coming," Henry said.

"Yeah, me too." Sammy scanned the end of the driveway, watching for Mr. John and the wagon.

Jack walked out on the porch and sat next to Henry. "So, your parents are coming today?"

"Yeah. I can't wait!" Henry's grin spread from ear to ear.

"No kidding." Jack smiled.

"Does anyone come to visit you, Jack?"

"Naw. But it's okay, I'm used to it. This is my fifth year here, and nobody's visited me yet."

Henry's heart sank. "It must be hard on you."

Jack shrugged. "It's not. The kids here are my family."

Off in the distance, Mr. John's baritone voice could be heard singing "Polly Wolly Doodle."[2] They stood and tried to catch a glimpse of the occupants of the wagon, their excitement growing. Sammy's face beamed when he caught sight of his mother and father. "There they are!"

Frances shrieked in delight, waving at her parents. "Mother, Father," she shouted.

A moment later Mr. John pulled on the reins. "Whoa, boys." The wagon rolled to a stop. The men climbed out first, then assisted the women off the wagon. Children jumped off the steps and into the arms of their parents.

---

2. Dan Emmett, "Polly Wolly Doodle," 1880.

"I guess Father and Kate are using the carriage," Henry said, disappointment tinging his voice. "I hope they get here soon."

"Don't worry, it won't be long," Ruth said, watching the end of the drive.

A few minutes later, the timeworn carriage turned off the main road. Hercules lumbered up the sandy drive. "It's Father and Kate!" Ruth blurted out.

Henry stood and squinted his eyes, trying to get a better view. "Father is by himself. Kate's not with him." As soon as the carriage stopped, they sprinted down the stairs and ran toward Herman. "Father!" Henry threw his arms around Herman.

"I sure have missed you!" Herman hugged Henry then turned to Ruth.

"Father!" She gave him a hug. Herman gave her a kiss on the cheek, noticing her sunburn.

"What happened, Ruthie? You're pink!"

"I was outside playing yesterday. The girls and I jumped rope for a long time."

"Okay. Good that you got the fresh air. Next time, though, you should try to stay in the shade."

"Yes, sir. Where is Kate?" Ruth asked.

"She's not feeling well and didn't think she could manage the ride here. She sends her love, though. So, you two, what are you showing me today?"

Henry spoke up, "We want to show you the barn. There's all kinds of stuff in it, like mice and cats. We can go to the pasture where the horses and cows are, too."

"Perhaps it's better that Kate's not here. I don't think she'd want to see any mice!" Herman chuckled.

....

Henry gave the door his best tug; it squeaked in protest as it opened. A ray of sunlight illuminated the aisle and specks of dust floated in the air, the rich, earthy smell of the hay greeting them. Tapping her tail on the ground, a calico cat showed her annoyance with the guests. She got up and darted around them and out the door. Henry turned to Herman. "She's only one of the cats that come in the barn. There's a bunch more." He pointed out the hayloft and the grain bins.

A mouse skittered across Ruth's path and into one of the horses' stalls. "Eeek!" Squealing, she jumped backward.

"There's nothing to be afraid of. They won't hurt you," Henry said.

"I still don't like them!"

Herman chuckled. "Didn't you say you wanted me to see the horses and cows?"

"Oh, yeah, they're in the pasture. C'mon." He led them to where the livestock were grazing. Pointing to each animal, he named them.

"Is there anything else you want to show me?"

"We showed you most everything last time." Henry scanned the grounds. "I guess we can go back in the woods if you want."

"How about next time?" Herman wiped his brow with his handkerchief.

"Okay, Father." Henry scuffed the ground with his foot.

"I know, we can sit under the trees at the picnic tables," Ruth said.

"That sounds delightful," Herman said.

The steady breeze was refreshing. They chatted for a few minutes before they couldn't hear each other for the sound of barking dogs. The pack galloped onto the playground. "There's Bella!" Ruth got up and went to her dog.

"Father?" Henry said.

"Yes?"

"Did you get my letter? I gave it to Miss Gertrude to mail a few days ago."

"No, I didn't get a letter. Sometimes it can take a while. I'm sure I'll receive it tomorrow."

"Oh, okay." Henry pressed his lips together and dropped his head. *Father doesn't know. Did Miss Gertrude even mail it?* Henry's heart pounded, the pit of his stomach burning. He brushed the perspiration off his forehead.

"Henry?"

"Uh, yes, Father?"

"Are you okay?"

"Yes, sir. I just got hot for a minute."

"You're sure?" Herman asked. Henry nodded.

The three chatted about home, Kate, Herman's work at the grocery store, and the two-week break at Christmastime. Herman checked the time. "Unfortunately, visiting time is over."

Henry dropped his head. "I'll miss you, Father."

"I'm going to miss you, too." Herman gave Henry a hug, holding him close. They walked back to the schoolhouse, the mood somber.

Herman found Eddy and David's parents, the Binghams, chatting with Alex Johnsen's parents on the front porch. "Oh, hello, Mr. and Mrs. Bingham; Mr. and Mrs. Johnsen. So nice to see you again," Herman said. They talked for a few minutes until Miss Gertrude came out on the porch. She looked at them with her ever-present frown. The parents made their way to the wagons to return home.

Herman walked to the driver's seat, then turned and gave both Henry and Ruth one last hug. "Keep writing letters, we enjoy reading them." He got aboard and turned Hercules around, clicking his tongue. Rolling down the driveway, the carriage headed home. Henry and Ruth waved until their father was out of sight.

"It was so nice to see him." Her voice quavered.

"Yeah," Henry said. They turned around and walked up the steps to the schoolhouse. "Where are you going?"

"I don't know, I might read. What about you?"

"Maybe take Buster for a walk. I'm not sure." Henry sat down on the top step. The contented feeling he had felt melted into sadness. Henry didn't hear the front door open.

14

"Good afternoon, Henry." The gravelly voice jarred him away from his thoughts.

"Uh, h-hi, Miss Gertrude."

"Did you enjoy your visit with your father?"

"Yes, ma'am. It was nice to see him."

"You must have had a lot to talk about." Raising her eyebrow, her lip curled.

"Um, yes m-ma'am. We talked about stuff at home, mostly. I showed him the cows and horses out in the pasture, too."

"Hm. Didn't talk about anything else, Henry?"

"No, ma'am." He mopped his brow with his sleeve.

"Very well. Be on time for supper." She went back into the schoolhouse and closed the door.

She knows! She knows I told Father! Why haven't I been punished? His head began to spin. He tried to push the thoughts out of his mind.

....

Mr. Dan opened the rear barn doors all the way and walked to the pasture gate, opening it. Henry watched the horses and cows trot into the barn. Peeking in, he saw the animals go to their stalls. Mr. Dan followed them in and bolted each door. "Wow, Mr. Dan. How did they know to go in the right stall?"

"They're smart. They know where their food is." He took off his Stetson and mopped his forehead with an old rag. He ran his fingers through his black hair before replacing his hat.

The horses pawed the ground, whinnying. "They must be hungry!" Henry went to the bin and scooped out the grain.

"Make sure you bolt the doors when you give them the hay and water," Mr. Dan said, leaving.

"Yes, sir."

Eddy slipped through the door. "Hey, Henry. So, I think Wednesday is the best night to go out in the woods. You going?"

Henry hesitated. "I guess so. Is Will coming with us?"

"I don't think so. He's too afraid." Eddy grinned.

"Well, I'm not afraid!" Henry said, trying to convince himself.

....

The aroma of freshly baked bread filled the air. Sammy's mouth watered. "Sure does smell yummy." The boys sat on the bench, waiting for supper. "Yay, chicken an' dumplings!" Sammy took in the delicious aroma when Miss Minnie placed the bowl in front of him.

She set a bowl in front of Henry, and he smiled. *Smells good, but not as good as Kate's.*

After supper the two boys went out on the front porch and sat on the steps. "Did you have a nice visit with your parents, Sammy?"

"I sure did. It was great to see them, but I miss them already."

"Yeah, I know what you mean. Two hours isn't much time." Henry picked up a long stick and drew shapes in the soft dirt at the bottom of the steps.

"My parents brought me somethin'!"

"What?" Henry dropped the stick.

"C'mon, I'll show you." Sammy and Henry jogged to the dorm.

Sammy opened his trunk and pushed the clothing to the side. He pulled out a drawstring bag and smiled. "Here it is!"

"Well, what is it? Show me!" Sammy opened the bag and let Henry peer in. "When can we play?"

Sammy turned the bag upside down, and marbles went everywhere. "Quick! Help me get 'em." Laughing, they scrambled to rein them in.

"We can't play in here, there's not enough space." Henry frowned.

"We can take them the next time we go out in the woods."

Henry's shoulders sagged. "We won't be able to go until next Saturday."

"Yeah, I know. I don't want to get caught, and have Miss Gertrude take them from me."

"Okay. Want to play slaps? Or we can go to the library and read."

"Let's go to the library. I need to find a new book. I'm almost done with *Robin Hood*,"[1] Sammy said.

....

Wednesday, September 13, 1905

"So, you're going out with us tonight, right?" Eddy dropped a scoop of grain into Zippy's bin.

"Yeah, but only if you're sure they won't catch us," Henry said.

"Naw, they won't. It's me, you, Sammy, and Jack. I'll come to your room about midnight to get you."

"Okay." Henry climbed the ladder to the hayloft and threw down the pads of hay. They finished up and went to the dorm.

"Hey, Sammy." Henry closed the door behind him.

"Hi. You ready for tonight?" Sammy grinned.

"Yeah, but I'm still nervous. What if the dogs start barking? Won't the grownups wake up?"

1. Howard Pyle, *The Adventures of Robin Hood*, 1883.

"Never did before. Don't worry about it. Everything will be all right. You'll have fun; we might get lucky and see a few animals. And no, I'm not talking about panthers and bears! Let's go eat, I'm hungry."

....

After supper Henry went to the library to read. Ruth and Lorene sat at one of the tables, chatting. "Hi," Ruth said, noticing her brother.

"Hi." Henry sat in one of the overstuffed chairs and opened his book. *I'm glad they're here. Maybe Miss Gertrude won't come in and talk to me.* He turned to chapter eight and began to read. Soon he was on a mission with Jim to deliver a letter to the one-legged Long John Silver. Wrapped up in his book, Henry didn't notice Ruth and Lorene had left the library.

He heard her heavy footsteps in the hallway; his stomach fluttered. "Hello, Henry." The raspy voice sent goosebumps down his spine.

Henry froze. "Um, hi, Miss Gertrude."

"Are you enjoying your book?"

"Yes, ma'am. It's *Treasure Island.*"

"An excellent story. You haven't asked me to mail any letters lately. Is something wrong?"

"Um, no, ma'am."

"I'm sure your father would love to hear from you. You should write to him soon."

"Yes, ma'am, I will." Her eyes were on him for a moment, but to Henry it was an eternity. She turned and walked away. *Why is she doing this?*

....

Sammy lay on his cot, reading. "Where have you been?"

"The library, reading. Want to play some cards?"

"Yeah, sure." Sammy dug the cards out of his trunk and shuffled them. "Are you getting excited about tonight? I am."

"Yeah, but I'm a little scared, too. I've never been out late at night."

"It'll be fun." The boys played until bedtime. "We need to try and get some sleep."

"All right." Henry lay in bed thinking about Miss Gertrude and how much she'd been talking to him. *She doesn't talk to the other kids as much as she has to me.* He couldn't find a comfortable position and had trouble falling asleep. Eventually the sound of rolling thunder and the steady rainfall lulled him to sleep.

....

"Hey, Sammy," Eddy whispered, nudging him. "Sammy."

Sammy stirred and groaned. "What is it?"

"It's me, Eddy. Let's go." The whispering woke Henry.

"What time is it?" Henry sat up.

"About twelve-thirty. Hurry up and put your clothes on. Jack is waiting for us."

"Okay." Sammy yawned.

....

The boys met up with Jack behind the barn. Moonlight reflected in a dozen shallow puddles, glittering in the night. Once on the main trail, Jack passed the second and third turn-offs and kept walking. "Where are we going?" asked Henry.

"We're heading to an area where there are a lot of oak trees—should be more animals there," answered Jack.

"What do you think we'll find?"

"No tellin'. Might see possums, raccoons, or skunks. Or maybe a gray fox or bobcat."

"Really? A fox or a bobcat?" Henry asked.

"Yeah, it's possible. I've heard them before but never seen either one." The boys walked until Jack stopped. "Let's go this way." The path was much narrower than the main trail, and they had to walk single file. Jack, in the lead, stopped and turned to face the others. He put his finger on his lips and his other hand went to his ear. *Waaahh, waaahh, waaahh, waaahh.* Jack pointed ahead and to the right, toward a large oak. There, on one of the branches, lay a bobcat. Eddy moved to get a better view, stepping on a branch. *Crunch.* The moonlight caught a flash of tan fur jumping to the ground and sprinting into the underbrush. "Did you see that? It was a bobcat! It was making the 'waaahh' sound," Jack said in a hushed voice.

"Wow, it's the first time I ever saw one!" Henry said.

"Yeah, me too!" Sammy grinned.

"Up the path is a clearing. Let's see if anything is there," Jack said. The boys were careful to not make any noise. Once in the clearing, they surveyed their surroundings. On the other side of the grassy area, they saw movement. Something black with a white stripe tottered along, with four smaller white-striped animals following. "Skunk!" Jack called out. "Go back!" The boys turned and scrambled back down the path. Sensing the disturbance, the big skunk went on the defense. Growling, she stood on her front legs and raised her tail, spraying her sharp, nauseating scent in the boys' direction.

"Whew! That was close," Sammy said, panting. The skunk's scent emanated through the woods. The overwhelming, noxious odor of rotten eggs filled their nostrils.

The boys backtracked down the trail to the third turn-off. "Let's go to the creek," Jack said. As they got closer, a chorus of gopher frog calls rang in their ears: *Rrreeee, rrreeee, rrreeee.*

"Wow, there must be a thousand of them." Henry said. The high-pitched call of the cicadas chimed in: *Zzziii, zzziiii, zzziiii,* the sound deafening. *Smack!* Henry slapped a mosquito.

"We don't want to get too close to the creek. I've seen water moccasins in it. They come out at night." Jack smashed a mosquito on his arm. "The mosquitoes are swarming." *Smack!* Henry hit another one.

"Yeah, there must be a million!" Eddy said, swatting one on his face.

Clouds moved across the moon, dimming its light. "Sure is dark out here," Henry whispered.

Guurrr, guurrr, guuurrrr. A deep, guttural growl came from across the creek, twenty yards away. Moving in the direction of the sound, the boys' eyes widened. The clouds parted, the moonlight reflecting off the golden eyes that were staring at them. The big cat crouched and hissed, showing its fangs. In a calm whisper, Jack told the boys to turn around. "Walk, don't run, back up the path." They reached the main trail and broke into a run. They didn't stop until they were almost out of the woods. Panting, they sat on the sandy ground to rest before heading back to the dorm.

"A panther! I can't believe we saw a panther!" Sammy said.

....

Thursday, September 14, 1905

"Ugh. Time to get up," Sammy complained.

"Huh? What?" Henry propped himself on his elbow. "The sun is barely up. I'm tired. I want to go back to sleep." Henry yawned, laying back down.

"C'mon. You don't want to be tardy for school."

"Okay." He sat on his cot, scratching his arms. Henry counted the mosquito bites. "I got bit six times. They itch like crazy."

"Don't let the grownups see you scratching them. With six bites, they'll know you've been outside at night."

Miss Fannie finished a lesson on grammar and instructed the students to read silently. Henry was glad the lesson was over. He had focused on his mosquito bites and not grammar. Henry opened his book and read, almost nodding off. He was relieved when the bell rang for dinner.

....

Eddy and Henry arrived at the barn early. Jack, Sammy, and Will were still cleaning stalls. "Hey, Will, me and Sammy will finish up," Jack said.

"Yeah, okay, thanks." Will hung the pitchfork on a rusty nail and headed for the dorm.

"So, Henry, what do you think? Did you have fun last night?" Jack asked.

"Yeah! I can't believe there was a panther out there!"

"It sure was special. It was only the second time I've seen one," Jack said. They chatted until Mr. Dan brought the cows and horses in from the pasture. Henry and Eddy wasted no time getting to work. They finished up quickly and scooted to the dorm.

Henry went to the bathroom and turned on the water. He scrubbed his forearms, trying to make the itchiness go away. It didn't help.

15

After supper, Miss Gertrude called Henry and a few others into the library. "Boys and girls, here are letters from your parents." When she handed Henry his letter, she held onto it for a split second. He looked up at her. "Here you go, Henry." Her frown turned into a twisted half-smile.

"T-Thank you, Miss Gertrude." She let go, and Henry's hand began to tremble. He glanced at Ruth. She was already reading her letter. Hesitating for a moment, he flipped it over and ripped it open. He took the letter out, smoothing out the folds. Henry felt a burning sensation in his throat as he read. He tried to swallow the smoldering lump but couldn't. Henry scanned the letter. Shuddering, he folded the letter and placed it back in the envelope. *Why didn't Father say anything about the punishment? She didn't mail it! But why haven't I been in trouble?* He struggled to make sense of it all. Henry wanted to talk to Sammy about his suspicions but didn't want to be scolded for writing the letter in the first place. *He'll say, "I told you so."*

....

Henry opened the door and found the room empty. He got his book and lay on his cot to read, scratching his mosquito bites until they were inflamed once again. "Ugh! I wish they'd stop itching!" Thoughts of Miss Gertrude haunted him, and he couldn't concentrate on his book. The door opened, startling him.

"Hey," Sammy said.

"Oh! Hi. What have you been doing?"

"Playing with my dog. We got some time before it's lights out. Want to play some cards?"

"Sure, I'll play." Henry was relieved to have a distraction from his discombobulated thinking.

"Jack showed me a new card game the other day. It's called hearts. Want to play?"

"Yeah, I'd like to try something different."

"It's fun. I think you'll like it." The boys played until nine o'clock. Henry crawled into bed. Tired from the night before, he welcomed the chance to sleep. Sammy put out the light, and Henry closed his eyes. He soon fell into a sleep tormented by nightmares.

....

"No, no, no!" Henry cried out in his sleep. "No, don't do it!" Henry bawled.

"Wake up, Henry!" Sammy shook him. "Henry!"

"No," Henry shouted. The sound of his own yelling woke him.

"Shh. It's okay. You were having a nightmare."

"Uh-uh-uh." Henry tried to calm his breathing. "I-It was horrible, Sammy. Miss Gertrude put me in the closet. She said I had to stay there for three days, and that I couldn't have any food or water."

"She's mean, but she would never leave a kid in the closet for three days. What made you dream somethin' that crazy?"

Henry wiped the tears from his eyes, "I don't know." He squirmed. He knew precisely why he had the nightmare. *She knows!*

"Think you can go back to sleep?"

"I'm not sure." Henry was afraid to sleep. Afraid he'd have more nightmares. He willed himself to stay awake, but the rhythmic sound of Sammy's breathing soothed him and soon he fell into a dreamless sleep.

....

Saturday, September 16, 1905

Eddy latched Zippy's stall door. "We're done for now. Where are you headed?"

"I don't know. Thinking about taking Buster on a walk. Might go back in the woods to where we saw the panther the other night. Want to go?" Henry asked.

"Yeah, sure." Eddy said.

"We can go in a few minutes. I'll ask Sammy if he wants to go."

"Okay."

....

Henry opened the door and found Sammy on his cot, reading. "Hey, want to take our dogs for a walk in the woods? Eddy's going."

Sammy's lip curled up. "How 'bout we take the marbles instead? I haven't had much of a chance to play with 'em yet."

"Yeah! It sounds like fun."

Henry and Sammy found Eddy sitting in the shade of the schoolhouse, playing with his dog. "Sammy's got something else he wants to take to the woods. C'mon," Henry whispered.

Eddy cocked his head and looked at Sammy. "What?"

Sammy glanced around, then took the bag out of his pocket. He opened it and showed the contents to Eddy. "Woo-hoo! I haven't played in a long time," he whispered. The boys walked behind the barn and into the woods.

They walked on the main trail until they got to the second turnoff. "Let's go this way," Sammy said. They came upon a sandy area, just big enough to play a game of marbles. Sammy picked up a twig and drew a circle in the sand. The boys played two rounds before deciding it was getting close to dinnertime. "C'mon boys, we got to go."

Eddy and Henry followed Sammy back up the path and onto the main trail. They opened the dormitory door as the bell rang. They had fifteen minutes to clean up and be in the dining hall. The boys were the last to arrive, sitting down seconds before Miss Gertrude came in and took a seat.

After dinner, Henry went to the library and opened his book to chapter thirteen: "How My Shore Adventure Began." He was swept up in the excitement, and for a moment he forgot about Miss Gertrude and Pinehurst.

"Hello, Henry." The gruff voice startled him. He snapped back into reality.

"Hi, Miss G-Gertrude." He swallowed.

"Enjoying your book?"

"Yes, ma'am."

"Come with me."

"Uh, yes, m-ma'am." He followed her through the classroom and into her office.

"Henry, please sit down." Miss Gertrude pulled out a chair. Sweat moistened his brow, and a drop dribbled down his spine. He shivered. She took a seat at her desk, directly in front of him. "Did you mention the punishment here at Pinehurst to your father?"

Henry hesitated. He opened his mouth to speak, then shut it before he answered. *This is a trap! If I say no, and she knows about my letter, I'll be in trouble for lying. If I say yes, I'll still get in trouble. What do I say?* Henry thought for a moment and chose his words deliberately, "I, um, I didn't tell my father."

She picked up on his nuanced words. "Well, either way, it appears you don't believe the rules apply to you. Do you remember last Sunday's Bible lesson?"

"Yes, ma'am." He wiped the sweat from his upper lip.

"Breaking rules here at Pinehurst is like breaking one of God's laws. The punishment for breaking one of His laws is eternal damnation. Quite severe, wouldn't you say?"

Henry's lips trembled. "Yes, m-ma'am."

"You broke an important rule, Henry. I'm disappointed in you." The searing heat of her stare burned through him like a branding iron. Miss Gertrude opened a drawer and took out an envelope. She handed it to him.

Henry's heart sank. He dropped it as if it were on fire. *This is my letter. She didn't mail it. Oh no! Please, God, help me!* He burst into tears. A wave of nausea swept through him.

"Henry, don't you realize if you follow the rules and do your best, I wouldn't need to punish you?"

"Yes, m-ma'am," Henry whimpered, his eyes brimming with tears.

"Your punishment for attempting to tell your father about what goes on here is five lashes with the strap and to spend two hours in the closet. I want to make sure you've got plenty of time to think about what you did."

Henry's stomach tightened. *No! This can't be happening!*

"I want you to place your hands on my desk." Shaking, he complied. Tears streamed down his face and splattered on her desk. She grasped the strap, walked over to him and moved the chair. Her barbarity was unmistakable as she raised the strap and brought it down on Henry's backside. *Smack!* "Owwww." Henry's body jerked into a standing position. He leaned over and placed his hands on the desk again. *Smack!* His eyes squeezed shut. He barely got a chance to suck in another breath of air before the strap hit again. *Smack!* After two more strikes, Henry's legs gave out, and he fell to his knees. Miss Gertrude pulled him to his feet.

"Time to go the closet and think about the rules and how to make the right choice. You made a poor decision when you tried to tell your father about the punishment here at Pinehurst. Come with me." Henry followed her to the dormitory. She headed toward the stairs but then walked around them. She stopped. Underneath the staircase was a door. Turning the knob, she opened it. "This is where you will remain for the next two hours. I will come back at quarter to five to let you out. I want you to think about how you can make better choices. In you go." She nodded toward the tiny room. He hesitated, then walked in.

The cramped space was dark. A narrow slice of light from under the door illuminated little. Henry's heart rate increased as he hyperventilated. He sobbed and shook uncontrollably. *Father, I need you.* Cradling his face in his hands, tears flowed. Henry thought about the times he got in trouble at home. *Father never hit me. And there are all the times Kate yelled at me. But none of it was really bad. Why does it have to be so horrible here?*

His heartbeat pounded in his head. *Make it stop!* Henry sniffed and wiped his nose with the back of his hand. He took deep, long breaths to try and calm himself. *If Miss Gertrude hadn't read my letter, none of this would've happened!* Time crawled. His thoughts jumped from one thing to the next. He shivered and thought about Sunday's Bible lesson. *Eternal punishment? God wouldn't do that. But why did he let me get punished today?* Confused, he closed his eyes and wept.

At four forty-five, Miss Gertrude opened the door. Henry stumbled out and almost fell. She grabbed him and steadied him. She held Henry's chin in her hand and turned his head toward her face. Their eyes locked. "Will you attempt to tell your father about the punishment and our extracurricular activities here at Pinehurst again, Henry?"

"N-No, ma'am."

"Very well, I'll hold you to your word." She walked him upstairs to the bathroom and instructed him to wash his face. "You have a few minutes before supper. Please make sure you're on time." She turned and walked down the stairs and out the door. Relieved from being out of the closet, and from not having to spend any more time with Miss Gertrude, he cupped his hands and took a drink of the cool water.

....

Henry hurried to the dining hall. He didn't want to be late, and he didn't want the others to see him walk in. He was the first to arrive. He took a seat and stared at the table.

Sammy came in and sat beside him. "What happened to you?" He furrowed his brow and leaned back to get a better view of Henry.

"I don't want to talk about it."

"Wow, were you punished?"

"I said I don't want to talk about it!"

"Okay, okay. You don't have to get mad."

Ruth and Lorene arrived and took the last two seats on the girls' side. Ruth glanced at Henry. She caught his eye and gave him a questioning look. He turned away. Miss Gertrude entered the hall and took her seat, and the buzz of conversation stopped. Thankful for the silence, Henry had a thirty-minute reprieve; he didn't want to talk to anyone.

After supper Henry jumped up and headed for the dorm. Ruth wanted to talk to him, but he was out the door before she could stop him. Once in the dorm, he kicked off his shoes and jumped into bed. Facing the wall, Henry hoped Sammy wouldn't come back to the dorm anytime soon. *I can't let them know what happened. They told me not to tell Father. I should've listened to them!*

To Henry's disappointment, Sammy came in and sat on his cot. "Hey, want to play some cards?"

"I don't feel like it."

"What's wrong with you?"

"Nothing."

"You sure are acting strange. I'm heading to the library to read."

Henry was thankful Sammy left. He wasn't ready to tell the truth, at least not yet. Tired from all the stress, Henry fell into a deep sleep and dreamed. He dreamt he was home, and it was Christmas morning. A towering fir tree stood in front of the plate glass window in the parlor, decorated with his mother's favorite ornaments. Carefully wrapped presents were tucked under its broad branches. He and Ruth sat in the armchairs while his father and mother handed out the gifts. His mother handed him a long, skinny present and smiled. "This is for you, Henry." He ripped open the present and squealed in delight. "It's the fishing pole! This is the best present I ever got!" A feeling of warmth came over his body. The dream faded, leaving him with a lightness in his chest.

He was roused from his sleep by the noise of a door shutting. "You sleeping in your clothes? It's almost time for lights out."

"Uh, um, no." Henry sat up. "Do I have time to wash my face?"

"Yeah, you got about fifteen minutes."

He washed his face; the warm feeling diminished leaving a knot in his stomach. Henry returned and put on his nightshirt. He lay on his side, praying he wouldn't be haunted by nightmares.

....

Sunday, September 17, 1905

After reciting the Lord's Prayer, Miss Gertrude said, "Today's lesson is a continuation of last week. We will pick up with Romans, chapter 13, verse 4: 'For he is the minister of God to thee for good. But if thou do that which is evil, be afraid; for he bears not the sword in vain: a revenger to execute wrath upon him that doeth evil.'" She closed her Bible. "Children, we have an evildoer among us. An evildoer who thought the rules here at Pinehurst did not apply to him." Miss Gertrude paused, letting the children ponder her words. Henry shuddered. "The rules are in place to teach you a lesson in good versus evil, and how to make the right choice. Those who choose evil and make the wrong choice are punished for their misdeeds." She cleared her throat. "Henry, stand up." Feeling lightheaded, he forced himself to stand, holding onto his seatback. "Please tell the others the poor choice you made in regard to breaking the rules."

"I, uh, t-tried to tell my father about the p-punishment and work," Henry mumbled.

"I'm not sure everyone heard you. Please speak up and say it again."

"I said, I tried to tell my father about the punishment and the work." Gasps were heard throughout the room. Ruth's eyes filled with tears. Sammy turned his head away and rubbed his neck. Jack gaped at Henry. Muffled gasps were heard throughout the room.

"Tell us about the punishment you received for your evil deed."

"I was hit with the strap five times and put in the c-closet."

"Will you attempt to tell your father again, Henry?"

"No, m-ma'am."

"Let this be a lesson to you all: misdeeds are dealt with severely. We will now sing 'Where He Leads Me.'[1] Miss Fannie, would you please play the tune?" The music filled the room with a delicate melody.

1. Ernest W. Blandy, "Where He Leads Me," 1890.

Their voices faltered as they sang the hymn, unable to give it their best effort. "Thank you, Miss Fannie." Turning her attention to the children, Miss Gertrude said, "I want to leave you with a final thought: It is better to do good and be praised than to do evil and be punished. You are dismissed." They stood and filed out of the classroom. Henry bolted for the dorm.

....

Henry jumped on his cot and faced the wall. A minute later the door opened, and Sammy came in. *Ugh. I don't want to talk to him.*

"Wow, Henry! I can't believe you did it. I'm kinda proud of you. That took a lot of guts."

Henry turned over and sat up. "Really? I can't believe it either." His voice quavered.

"When did you tell him? During your last visit?"

"No, I wrote to him a couple of weeks ago. Miss Gertrude never mailed my letter. She kept it and read it."

"Wow. You mean she knew it this whole time and just punished you yesterday?"

"Yeah. She'd been acting strange toward me. She was too nice. I thought she might have read it."

"Hey, I know you feel bad. Want to play some cards? It might cheer you up."

"Yeah, okay." Henry slid off the cot and onto the floor. The boys played until the bell rang for dinner.

....

Once seated at the large dining table, Henry glanced at Ruth. She was staring at him with a furrowed brow. She mouthed the word, "Why?" He turned away but couldn't escape the stares. Many were whispering; Henry knew they were talking about him. He ate, staring at his plate. When Miss Gertrude dismissed them, he tried to leave the dining hall as quickly as possible. The others were in no hurry and jammed up the doorway. Henry squeezed his way through the crowd and into the hall. Ruth caught him by the back of his shirt. "Henry! Come here!" She pulled him toward the library. He was dreading this. He didn't want to talk to his sister. "What were you thinking?" She pushed him into one of the chairs.

"I did it because it's the only way out of here."

"But you're still here! Didn't you think about the consequences?"

"I want to go home, Ruth. This place is a nightmare!"

"I agree. But telling Father will only cause you more trouble. It won't get you anywhere."

"I'll think of something. You can't tell me every kid who's ever been here didn't tell his parents!"

"Yeah, maybe they did. And they got punished like you did."

"I don't want to argue with you, and I don't want to talk about it anymore."

Ruth's demeanor softened. "Okay. Please follow the rules. It hurts me when you're punished."

"I'm going to the dorm." He headed for the door. A single tear trickled down Ruth's cheek.

....

Bored, Henry headed for the barn at quarter to four. Sammy, Jack, and Will were still working. Hearing their voices, he stopped short of going inside. He stood outside the door and eavesdropped.

"Can you believe Henry tried to tell his father? He must be brave. I don't think I could do what he did," Jack said.

"Yeah, I thought for sure he wouldn't do it after telling Miss Gertrude that he would tell his father. He said she dared him to. I guess that's why he did it. He sure has guts. Have to give him that," Sammy said.

They think I'm brave? Wow. Henry's chest puffed out a little. Not wanting the boys to notice him, he slipped back to the dorm and waited for Eddy to come out. "You ready?"

"Yeah, let's go." The older boys were finishing up when the boys got to the barn. Henry and Eddy waited for Mr. Dan to bring in the animals.

"Hey, Henry, so you wrote a letter to your father telling him of the punishment here?"

Henry rolled his eyes. He'd had enough talking about what had happened. "Yeah, I did."

"Didn't you think Miss Gertrude would read the letter? I think she reads all the letters before she mails them."

Henry had not considered this. "I thought it was possible, but I didn't think she'd do it. Can we stop talking about it?"

"Yeah, sure." Eddy went up the ladder to the hayloft while Henry dropped the grain in the animals' bins.

16

Tuesday, September 19, 1905

Henry and Eddy barely got into the barn when they heard someone screaming. "Who is that?" Henry said.

"I'm not sure. Sounds like it came from behind the schoolhouse," Eddy said. The boys jogged out of the barn and surveyed the grounds. "Over there! At the chicken coop." They ran over to find out what was going on.

"What happened?" Henry asked, eyeing the bloody chick flapping around at Grace's feet.

Between sobs, she said, "I went to g-get the water. I left the gate open. A chick got out. One of the d-dogs ran up and g-got it!" Grace choked out the words. "He didn't k-kill it, b-but it's hurt real bad."

The back door to the schoolhouse slammed behind Miss Gertrude. She stomped her way over to the children. "What happened here?" Her nostrils flared.

"It was an accident. I-I left the gate open. He got out. A d-dog ran up and bit him," Grace wailed.

"You can't let it suffer. Pick it up and come with me." Miss Gertrude led Grace over to the chopping block. "Lay him on here." Grace's hands shook as she did what she was told. "Take this," she said, handing the trembling girl a hatchet. Miss Gertrude held the chick down on the block. "You have to put him out of his misery. I want you to take the hatchet and strike him right behind his head."

"I-I c-can't!" Grace could barely speak.

"You must. Now do it!" Miss Gertrude's eyes narrowed.

Grace squeezed the tears from her eyes. She lifted the hatchet with both hands, shaking. Down it went, hitting its mark. Blood spurted out onto the block. Grace let out an anguished howl and dropped the hatchet, falling to her knees.

Miss Gertrude hung the chick upside down on a wire to let the blood drain out. "You're not finished yet."

She walked Grace to the kitchen. "Miss Minnie, I need you to boil a pot of water. Grace has a chick to pluck."

Miss Minnie glared at the girl. "I'll get it started now." She pointed at the trembling girl. "You, there. Go sit at the table in the corner." Still bawling, Grace tottered to the table. When the water came to a boil, Miss Minnie said, "Go get the chicken." Grace slid off the chair and went outside. Her hand shook as she took the headless chick from the wire. Holding the carcass at arm's length, she returned to the kitchen and handed it to the frowning woman. Holding it by the feet, Miss Minnie dunked it in the scalding water to loosen the feathers. After a few dunks, she placed it in the sink to cool off. The stench of the scalded feathers filled the room. Grace put her hand over her mouth and nose but couldn't escape the sickening odor.

Miss Minnie placed a cloth on the large worktable and told Grace to have a seat. Placing the chick on the cloth, she showed the trembling girl how to pull the feathers out. "You need to get all of them off. Do you have any questions?" Grace shook her head. The tears began to flow again. She gripped a few feathers and cringed. Tugging on them, they slid out. She grasped more and pulled, ignoring the nausea that was building in her stomach.

"M-Miss Minnie? I think I'm f-finished."

Miss Minnie examined the chick. "Yes, that's good enough. I'll finish it up. Go get cleaned up and go to class."

"Y-Yes, ma'am."

....

Miss Fannie had just finished a grammar lesson and asked the students to read silently when Grace entered the classroom. Oblivious to the stares, Grace went to her seat, opened her book, and gazed at the page, not reading a word.

Clang. Clang. The students put their books away and prepared to go to the dining hall. "Please line up, children," Miss Fannie said. Grace did not move. Miss Fannie went to her and whispered, "Are you okay, Grace?" Jumping at the teacher's voice, she gazed at Miss Fannie with a blank expression. "Let's go, dear." Miss Fannie helped Grace out of her seat.

"I don't want to go to dinner," the fragile girl said.

"You must eat, Grace. It will make you feel better."

"I'm not hungry," Grace whispered.

"Maybe you'll change your mind. You must try to eat," Miss Fannie said, her eyes softening.

The students took a seat and waited for dinner to be brought in. Miss Minnie and Miss Nellie delivered plates with ham sandwiches and an orange to everyone, except for Grace. The children glanced at each other with puzzled looks. Miss Gertrude walked through the kitchen door, carrying a plate. She set it in front of Grace, then took her seat at the head of the table.

Grace's eyes flew open. "No, no, no!" she cried out, gagging. Everyone's eyes were on Grace and her plate. Henry, at the other end of the table, couldn't tell what was in front of her. He jabbed Eddy with his elbow and mouthed, "What is it?"

Eddy peeked at Grace and her plate. His eyes went wide. He whispered to Henry, "That's a little chicken on her plate. It's the one from this morning!" Eddy covered his mouth with his palm and swallowed.

Miss Gertrude gave thanks. "You may begin eating." Grace eyed her plate, shaking, her stomach churning. She didn't touch her food. "Grace, you must eat your dinner. It is sinful to waste food." Grace picked up her fork and jabbed at the meat on her plate. She broke a piece off. Squinting at it, her lips trembled. A sheen of perspiration covered her forehead. "Eat your dinner, Grace!" Miss Gertrude insisted.

Guiding the fork toward her mouth, her hand shook. She closed her eyes tight and took a bite. Her stomach rolled, then dropped. All of a sudden, her belly quivered. Without warning, she retched, covering her plate in vomit. Jumping up, she ran out of the dining hall. Miss Gertrude, not missing a beat, went after her. Stunned, the rest of the students wondered what had just happened. Two minutes later Miss Gertrude returned to the dining hall, half walking, half dragging the girl behind her. "Grace, you have spoiled your food. Take your plate in the kitchen and help Miss Minnie clean it." Miss Gertrude pursed her lips. With one hand covering her mouth, Grace carried the plate to the kitchen.

Miss Minnie glimpsed the plate and frowned. She handed the girl a spoon and placed the garbage bin in front of her. Scowling at Grace, she said, "Scrape this mess into the bin." Recoiling, Grace took the spoon and began to push the chicken and vomit into the bin. "Now you need to take it to the sink and wash it with soap." Grace cleaned the plate, fighting off the nausea that enveloped her.

....

The students returned to the classroom and had a depressing afternoon. No one wanted to listen to Miss Fannie teach the day's math lesson, especially Grace. Miss Fannie knew all too well that she wouldn't be able to get much accomplished for the rest of the day. "Children, let's go outside and take a break."

The students jumped out of their seats to line up and were out the door in a flash. Relieved to be outside, the children took advantage of the jump ropes, swings, and balls. Grace went to an empty picnic table and took a seat. She folded her arms on the table and cradled her head. Ruth noticed and felt badly for the girl. "Hi, Grace." Ruth sat beside her. Grace kept her head down. "I'm sorry about the chick. Is there anything I can do for you?"

Grace sat up. "It was an accident! I didn't mean for it to get out of the chicken run. One of the dogs got hold of it and bit it really bad." Tears streamed down her cheeks.

"I know you didn't mean for it to happen. All we can do when we make mistakes is to learn from them. That's what my father says. I think he's right." Ruth placed a hand on Grace's arm. Grace looked at Ruth and said nothing. She went back to cradling her head in her arms, her tears dripping onto the picnic table. Ruth put her hand on Grace's back, giving her gentle pats.

Miss Fannie, annoyed with Miss Gertrude and her unbelievable punishments, decided to give the children a long break outside. The children were delighted and enjoyed their extended playtime. Miss Fannie went to the picnic table where Grace sat. Sitting next to the girl, she put her arm around her. "Are you okay, Grace? I know you've had a horrible day."

Lips trembling, tears welled up in Grace's eyes. She sniffed and shrugged her shoulders. Miss Fannie took out a handkerchief and dabbed at the corners of Grace's eyes. Crying, her small body shook. "Shh. It will be okay, Grace. I promise." But she knew full well it wouldn't be okay. Closing her eyes, she gave Grace a squeeze.

That evening at supper, the mood in the dining hall was somber. The children picked at their meals; no one had an appetite. Grace felt numb; bile bubbled up in her throat quashing her appetite.

····

Henry sat in one of the overstuffed chairs, while Sammy, Eddy, and Jack sat at a table. "Poor Grace," Henry said.

"Yep, she got it pretty bad today. I feel sorry for her," Eddy said.

Jack glanced around the room. In a hushed voice, he said, "Miss Gertrude is evil."

"She sure is," Sammy agreed. "How'd she get like that, anyway?"

"I don't know. She's been like that since I first came here," Jack said.

"She scares me," Henry said, shivering.

"I think she wants us all to be scared," Sammy said, shaking his head.

····

Saturday, September 23, 1905

After feeding the horses and cows, Eddy and Henry sat out back of the schoolhouse brushing their dogs and talking about Grace and the chick. "That's got to be the worst punishment ever," Henry said.

"Yeah, it was pretty bad. I think I'd rather get whipped a hundred times than to do what Grace had to do." Eddy shivered.

Miss Gertrude opened the back door and stood on the threshold. "Boys, please put the brushes away and come with me." Henry's heart rate quickened. She held the door open and waited for them to put the brushes away. They followed her down the hall.

"What did we do?" Henry mouthed. Eddy shrugged his shoulders. Miss Gertrude walked into the library. Jack and Sammy were sitting at one of the tables.

"Have a seat, boys." Henry bit his lower lip. "Mr. John is taking you to the river today to catch fish for tonight's supper." Henry looked at the others and gaped in amazement. The group gave a quiet cheer. "Miss Nellie has packed dinners for you. Jack and Sammy, Mr. John will make sure you're back in time to clean the stalls. Be ready to leave in fifteen minutes."

Mr. John pulled Ajax and Apollo to a stop at the front of the schoolhouse. "Les' go, boys." They scrambled off the porch and into the wagon. The old man clicked his tongue, and the big bays pulled the wagon down the drive and onto the main road.

"Woo-hoo!" Jack hooted. "I haven't been fishing in a long time."

"Me either!" Eddy said, grinning.

Ajax and Apollo settled into a comfortable rhythm. "We be headin' south to Remington. It's the closes' place for catfish 'round here. Take us about forty-five minutes to get there. I'm gonna teach y'all a song. One o' my favorites. It's called 'The Flying Trapeze.'[1] I'll teach you the chorus first." Mr. John began singing:

> "He'd fly through the air with the greatest of ease,
> That daring young man on the flying trapeze . . ."

Mr. John continued singing the chorus. "Okay, boys, now sing along with me." He sang the chorus again. The boys stumbled through the words. "Les' sing it again!" The boys joined in and they sang with fewer mistakes. "Okay, now for the first verse." Mr. John sang, and the boys got it on the third try. By the time they got to the fishing spot, they knew the first two verses and the chorus by heart and sang right along with Mr. John. Just beyond Remington, Mr. John pulled the horses

1. George Leybourne, "The Flying Trapeze," 1867.

to a stop next to a clearing. The boys gathered the cane poles and bait bucket and jumped off the wagon. "We gonna be catchin' catfish today. Any o' you done catch them before?"

"Yes, sir, Mr. John, I have!" Henry beamed.

"I've caught a few," Jack said.

"Yeah, me too," Sammy added.

"I've caught fish in the river before, but not catfish," Eddy said.

"We got us some expert fishermen here!" Mr. John said, chuckling. "We gonna start with night crawlers for bait. If they don't work, we'll try the chicken liver. Get a pole an' follow me." Mr. John picked up the bait bucket and a basket and walked down to the riverbank. "Here's the best place fo' catfish. See how the river bends some here? The water digs a hole when it flows by, makin' the perfect spot for 'em." Mr. John held out the bucket, and each boy took out a squirming worm. "Bait your hooks an' then watch me." Mr. John got his pole ready and held it out by his side and cast his line. "Now let it settle for a minute. Gotta tug on it a little from time to time. Now spread out, y'all. Don't want nobody to ge' hit with a pole."

By two o'clock the fishermen had filled the basket with catfish. "I think we done caught enough. C'mon y'all, time to wrap it up." The boys gathered their poles and headed for the wagon. Sammy went back for the bait bucket and glanced around to make sure they got everything. "We all set?" Mr. John said.

"Yes, sir, Mr. John," Jack said, taking a seat. Ajax and Apollo pulled the wagon back onto the road and headed for Pinehurst. A few minutes before three o'clock, the wagon turned off the main road and onto the circular drive. The mood went from cheerful to gloomy as soon as the schoolhouse came into view. Mr. John guided Ajax and Apollo behind the barn and unhitched them from the wagon. Jack and Sammy went to the barn. Mr. John pointed to Henry and Eddy. "Y'all take the fish to Miss Minnie."

"Yes, sir, Mr. John," Henry said. They picked up the basket and headed for the kitchen.

Henry knocked on the kitchen door with his free hand. Miss Minnie opened the door and told the boys to put the basket on the oversized worktable. "Do either of you know how to clean catfish?"

"I do," Henry said.

"I'll need your help. First we have to wash off the fish. Here's a knife you can use. Put the fillets on the platter and the rest in here." Miss Minnie placed a small basket on the table.

"Yes, ma'am," Henry said. Eddy helped Henry take the heavy basket of fish to the double sink. He got the water going, then washed each fish. Henry took the knife and slit one down its belly. His thoughts meandered to the time he left a fishy mess at home. *Kate sure was mad at me.* He thought about the punishment he received: not being able to see Thomas for two weeks. *And I thought that was bad. Ha!* He cleaned the fish and got most of them done before four o'clock. "Miss Minnie? I need to go to the barn and feed the animals now."

"Very well. I can finish up." Miss Minnie shuffled to the table and took the knife from him. Henry washed his hands, then ran to the barn.

....

Sunday, September 24, 1905

After dinner, Henry and Ruth went to the library. "I can't believe this change in you! You seem like your old self," Ruth said.

"Yeah, it's been a long time since I've felt this way. We caught about thirty. Sammy caught the most. Eddy caught the biggest one. It was about fifteen inches long. We sure had a great time. I hope we can do it again."

"I hope so too, Henry. What do you think we should do with Father and Kate today?"

"I don't know. We can show them the creek. We didn't go the last time we took them in the woods."

"I doubt if Kate would want to go. You and Father could go to the creek, and Kate and I can sit at one of the picnic tables and talk. There'd still be time for me to visit with Father."

"Okay. I'll ask Father when they come."

Gathering on the porch, the children waited for their parents to arrive. Just before one o'clock, Henry and Ruth heard Hercules snort as he headed up the driveway. "It's them!" Henry bounced on his toes in excitement. The carriage groaned to a stop.

"Hello, you two!" Herman gave them each a hug. He walked over to the passenger's side and helped Kate out of the carriage. She adjusted her hat and turned to walk around the wagon when Henry plowed into her, giving her a big hug.

"I've missed you," Henry said.

"I've missed you, too, dear." Kate gave Henry a warm smile. Ruth gave her a gentle hug and told Kate she was glad to see her.

"Well, you two, what's on the agenda for today?" Herman asked.

"Henry wants to take you to the creek today. Kate and I can sit at one of the picnic tables and talk while you're in the woods."

....

Henry and his father's steps were softened by the spongy crunch of the rust-colored pine needles which littered the trail. The fresh aroma of pine filled the air. They passed the gopher tortoise burrows and kept walking. "How far is the creek?"

"It's not much farther. Guess what I did yesterday!"

"Hm, caught a spider and put it in Ruth's hair?" Herman chuckled.

"No! I went fishing!"

"In the creek?"

"No, sir. Mr. John took Sammy, Jack, Eddy, and me to the river! We caught catfish for last night's supper."

"That sounds like fun. How many did you catch?"

"I caught eight! It's the most I ever caught at one time. Mr. John took us to a special place that has lots of them. We caught about thirty yesterday."

"My goodness, that's a lot of fish. I'm glad you had a good time."

"Yeah, I hope we can go again." A touch of melancholy tinged his voice. They took the third path and arrived at the creek within minutes. "It goes into the St. Johns. Sammy said there's not any big fish in it, but there are crawdads. They're sort of like shrimp. He says they taste like fish."

"Did you catch any?"

"No, we only saw the one." Henry pointed to an area on the other side. "We were here the other day and saw a few deer. We were whispering, and I guess they heard us. The deer got scared and ran away into the woods."

"You sure were close to them. I bet it was exciting."

"Yes, sir, it was!"

"I think we ought to head back now. I want to spend some time with Ruthie."

....

Yellow-brown leaves floated down from the oak, the breeze scattering them across the lawn. Herman and Henry joined Kate and Ruth at the picnic table. They talked about the garden and the dogs, and what they'd been learning in school. "Henry, how have you been?" Kate asked.

"I went fishing yesterday! Mr. John took me and three other boys to the river to catch catfish for last night's supper. I caught eight of them!"

"Well, it sounds like you enjoyed yourself."

"I sure did. I'm the only one who knows how to clean fish, so they let me do it. I got most of them done before Miss Minnie took over. And guess what?"

"I don't know."

"I didn't leave a mess!" Henry smiled.

Kate gave his arm a little squeeze. "I'm so proud of you."

Herman checked his watch. "We've got about fifteen minutes." They walked back to the schoolhouse and into the library. "Well, hello, Miss Gertrude. So nice to see you again."

Miss Gertrude's frown relaxed. "Hello, Mr. Conrader, Mrs. Conrader. How are you?"

"We are doing fine, thank you. Appears things are going well around here."

"Yes, Mr. Conrader, they are. You have two outstanding children. I'm pleased they are here at Pinehurst."

"Thank you. What a nice thing to say. We enjoy our visits with them. I wish we could come every week."

"I understand. We look forward to your next visit. Please excuse me, there is something I need to attend to."

"Certainly. It was nice to see you."

"My pleasure, Mr. Conrader."

17

Herman and Kate said their goodbyes to Henry and Ruth. The carriage made its way down the drive, Herman and Kate waving goodbye one more time. Turning his attention back to driving the carriage, Herman said, "Henry sure was excited. He does love his fishing."

"Yes, he does. It seems like they've become accustomed to being at Pinehurst."

"I agree. I hope they don't become too used to it. I want them back home someday!" Herman chuckled.

Kate smiled. "I do, too. It appears Henry has grown up a bit since our last visit. Did you hear him say he didn't leave a mess when cleaning the fish yesterday? It sounds like he's taking some responsibility for his behavior."

"Yes, I did notice it. I think you were right about Pinehurst. It does seem like a good fit for Henry."

....

Henry and Ruth walked into the schoolhouse and went to the empty library. "Can you believe what Miss Gertrude said, Ruth? We're outstanding, and she's happy to have us here? That may be true for you, but not me! She is such a liar!"

"Shhh, Henry! She might hear you."

"I still think we need to tell Father."

"Henry, you know it's a bad idea!"

"But what can we do? I don't want to stay here!"

"I don't know. Maybe we can figure out something when we go home at Christmastime."

"Christmas is a long time from now! I can't wait three months!"

"Henry, calm down. Getting upset won't help anything."

A sense of frustration filled Henry. "I want out now!"

....

Wednesday, September 27, 1905

"Hey, do you know what tonight is?" Eddy asked.

"No, what?" Henry said.

"It's the new moon!"

Henry waited until Mr. Dan brought in the animals and left, then said, "What's a new moon? Never heard of it." Henry began scooping out the cows' grain.

"It's where there is no moonlight at all. It's super dark, and you can see millions of stars. Sometimes there's even shooting stars! I asked Sammy and Jack, and they want to go outside tonight. Want to go?"

"I don't know."

"You're not afraid of the dark, are you?"

"No, I don't want to get in trouble, that's all."

"Yeah, sure. You're scared of the dark!" Eddy called out, climbing the ladder to the hayloft.

"Am not!"

"Prove it! Come out with us."

"Okay. I'll do it." The boys finished their work and went to the dorm.

....

Opening the door to his room, Henry said, "Hi, Sammy. So you're going out tonight to see the stars?"

"Yeah, are you?"

"I told Eddy I was, but I don't know. I'm afraid we'll be caught and get in trouble."

"I done it a few times and never got caught. It'll be okay, they won't know we're out there. We won't go far; we'll be out near the pasture where there's no trees to block our view."

"It sounds like fun." Henry hesitated; "Yeah, I'll go."

....

Eddy opened the door to room number four. "Henry. Wake up, it's me, Eddy." Henry stirred. "Wake up," Eddy repeated. Henry opened his eyes and blinked.

"Yeah, okay," Henry whispered. Sammy yawned and sat up.

"C'mon, let's go," Eddy said. Sammy and Henry got dressed. They crept down the stairs and left the dorm, heading toward the barn. They met up with Jack and slipped around the barn in the direction of the pasture.

"Sure is dark out here," Henry whispered.

"We need to be extra quiet. We don't want to stir up the dogs or wake up Mr. John and Mr. Dan," Jack said. They found a grassy area and lay down. "If we're lucky, there'll be a shooting star."

Eddy pointed out the Big Dipper. "Below the Big Dipper is the Little Dipper." He traced out the shape with his finger. "And at the end of the handle is the North Star."

"They only thing I see is a bright patch with dark spots," Henry spoke in a hushed voice. "I can't tell what you're looking at."

"The 'bright patch' is the Milky Way Galaxy. Those are millions of stars."

"How do you know so much, Eddy?" Sammy asked.

"I like to read books on astronomy. There's one!" Eddy pointed to the southern sky. "A shooting star!"

"Wow!" Sammy said. The boys watched the night sky in hopes of glimpsing another one.

"We've been here for a while. We need to go back to the dorm now," Jack said.

"Aw, I didn't get to see one," Henry said.

"Maybe next time. C'mon, let's go," Jack said. They stood and turned to leave. *Grrrrr.* The boys stopped and froze. *Grrrrr.* Bruiser, Mr. Dan's Rottweiler mix, stood before them, growling. "I'll distract him, and you three go back to the dorm. Don't run. Walk quickly and quietly."

"But you'll get caught," Eddy said.

"Do it!" Jack hissed.

When the three boys reached the dormitory door, Bruiser's growl turned into a ferocious bark, starting off a chain reaction of barking with the other dogs. They bolted upstairs and went to their rooms. "I sure hope Jack doesn't get caught," Henry said.

"He will. Mr. Dan will catch him, and he'll tell Miss Gertrude in the morning," Sammy whispered.

Jack talked Bruiser down and he stopped barking but continued to growl. Mr. Dan came out of his shack and got Bruiser to back off. "What are you doing out here in the middle of the night, boy?"

"I thought I heard somebody out here and I came out to see who it was."

Mr. Dan raised his lantern and stared into Jack's eyes. "You know you ain't supposed to be out here at night! Now git on back to the dorm. And don't do it again."

"Yes, sir!" Jack scooted to the dorm and didn't look back. He crept up the stairs, not knowing if Bruiser's barking had awakened any of the adults. Jack made it to his dorm room and closed the door without a sound.

....

Thursday, September 28, 1905

Miss Fannie introduced a grammar lesson on vowels. Jack only half-listened, expecting to be yanked out of class and into Miss Gertrude's office. He waited, knowing the whipping was coming. The door at the front of the room opened, and Miss Gertrude came out. Jack stiffened in his seat. The others watched her stop at Jack's desk and cast her eyes down at him. She gave him a long look, then glared at the others before leaving.

....

Friday, September 29, 1905

"Good morning, students. Yesterday we had a lesson on the different sounds each vowel can make. Today I would like to test what you learned. I will write ten words on the blackboard. You will copy them down and mark the sounds of the vowels." Miss Fannie listed them on the board. "When you are done, please raise your hand so I can check your work."

Henry yawned and stared at the blackboard. *I don't remember her talking about some of these kinds of words yesterday. She must've talked about them when Miss Gertrude walked through the room. What am I going to do?* He scanned the classroom: students were busy writing the words on their slates. Henry copied the words, leaving spaces to mark the vowels. He marked the ones he knew and stared at the ones he didn't. His stomach fluttered. I can't finish it all. I won't be able to raise my hand! He glanced at Miss Fannie. She sat at her desk flipping through papers. His gaze drifted to Sammy, then to his slate. He glanced at the teacher. She was still at her desk. He sat up and leaned forward, eyeing Sammy's slate. It was difficult to see, but he managed to glimpse some of what Sammy had written. He glanced again at Miss Fannie, then back to Sammy's slate. His eyes began to ache from staring to the side while facing front. Wrapped up in looking at the words and marks, Henry didn't notice Miss Fannie was no longer at her desk.

"Henry?"

He froze, turning his eyes back to his own slate. "Yes, ma'am?"

Miss Fannie walked from behind his desk and stood in front of him. "Can you explain to me why you were looking at Sammy's slate?"

"Uh, um. No, ma'am."

"Copying someone else's work is against the rules. Did you forget?"

The icy finger of fear gripped his chest. "Um, no, ma'am. I didn't forget."

"Then you will explain to Miss Gertrude why you broke one of our rules." The others were silent, listening to every word. Ruth shook her head. Miss Fannie walked to the front of the room and knocked on Miss Gertrude's office door. A moment later both ladies walked into the classroom.

Henry began to whimper, his heartbeat hammering in his ears as Miss Gertrude approached his desk. *Oh no! No, no, no!*

"Henry, come with me." Her eyes narrowed.

He stood, his legs giving out. She caught him and assisted him to her office. The children watched her half walk, half drag him to the front of the room and into her office.

....

"Well, Henry. I understand you copied Sammy's slate to do your work. Is that correct?"

"Y-Yes, ma'am," Henry whimpered.

"Why, Henry? You know it's against the rules." Miss Gertrude's steely eyes bore through him. "I want you to sit here for a few minutes until you can calm down."

He sat in a chair across from her massive cherrywood desk. She caressed the strap that hung from her neck. *How can I calm down?* He blinked. Black spots clouded his vision. Henry squeezed his eyes shut as his thoughts pounded in his head. *Why did I do it? Now I'm in trouble!*

"It's time, Henry. Stand and place your hands on the desk." Miss Gertrude slipped the strap from around her neck. She struck his backside five times, Henry crying out with each smack of the strap. "You've been in trouble three times in less than a month. That's unacceptable. For this reason, you will spend one hour in the closet."

With his stomach rolling, Henry's fear turned to dread. He scuffed his feet on the path on the way to the dorm. "I'll be back in one hour to let you out. I want you to think about the poor choices you've made over the last month." She shut the door, casting the closet into blackness. Henry broke out in a sweat as the darkness enfolded him.

At eleven-thirty, the door opened. Miss Gertrude frowned. "Henry, I want you to come back to my office with me. He blinked, his eyes adjusting to the light. She followed him to the schoolhouse.

"Have a seat." Miss Gertrude sat at her desk, across from him. "Did you think about the choices you made?"

"Yes, ma'am."

"What can you do differently next time?"

Henry searched his mind for an answer. "Uh, I'm not sure."

"You don't know? Well, I believe you need to think about it, Henry. In the meantime, I'll be watching you." Henry squirmed. With her stare fixed on him, his skin tingled as sweat prickled his forehead. *Tick. Tick. Tick. Tick. . . .* the sound of the clock filled his ears. "It's time for dinner, Henry."

All eyes were on Henry as he sat down. He kept his gaze down to avoid eye contact with the others, especially Ruth. Henry didn't want to have to deal with her. After dinner, Ruth managed to get close enough to him to grab his arm before they entered the classroom. "We need to talk. Go to the library after supper!"

He pulled away from her grip. "I have nothing to say."

....

As soon as class was over, Jack went to the barn. Mr. Dan had Zippy tied in the center aisle, trimming and filing the horse's hooves.

"Can I ask you something, Mr. Dan?"

"Yeah, what do you want?" Leaning over, he held one of Zippy's back hooves between his knees. Mr. Dan took out the large rasp and filed the rough edges on his left hoof.

"Why didn't you tell Miss Gertrude I was outside the other night?"

Mr. Dan dropped the hoof and stood. "I didn't want you to get in trouble. Simple as that."

"That's real nice of you, Mr. Dan. Thanks."

"You're welcome. Don't do it again—I might not be so nice next time."

"Yes, sir." Jack smiled. He got a pitchfork and a wheelbarrow and went to work cleaning stalls. Sammy and Will came in and joined him.

Jack hung the rake on the wall as Henry and Eddy entered the barn. "Hi, boys."

"What are you so happy about?" Eddy asked.

"I saw Mr. Dan when I got to the barn. He said he didn't want me to be in trouble, so he didn't tell Miss Gertrude about the other night. So he let me go."

"Wow. I never would've thought he'd do that," Eddy said. "You're lucky!"

"Yep," Jack said, walking out the door. Mr. Dan let the animals in the barn.

Eddy waited for Mr. Dan to leave. "Boy, Henry, you sure messed up this time!"

"What do you mean?"

"I'm talking about you looking at Sammy's slate!"

"I wouldn't have had to if Miss Gertrude didn't interrupt the grammar lesson."

"What are you talking about?" Eddy stared at Henry in disbelief. "Miss Gertrude didn't make you look at his slate! You got in trouble for cheating. The rest of us were distracted by her, too, but we didn't copy someone else's work." Henry began to protest, then stopped. "C'mon, let's finish," Eddy said.

....

"Hi," Henry said, opening his dorm room door.

"Hey. So you were copying my work, were you?" Sammy closed his book and sat up.

"I had to! I didn't know the answers. What was I supposed to do? Miss Gertrude distracted me yesterday, and I didn't hear what Miss Fannie was saying. If she hadn't come into the classroom, there wouldn't have been a problem."

Sammy laughed. "You tell yourself all kinds of things. You cheated!" Henry gaped at Sammy. "You can't blame Miss Gertrude! You did it to yourself." Henry was getting mad, and he flopped down on his cot and faced the wall.

"She said she would keep her eye on me," Henry mentioned as an afterthought.

"She did? Wow. You need to be extra careful. You can ask Jack about it. Last year, Miss Gertrude said the same thing to him. He kept getting in more and more trouble." Henry turned around and sat up. His stomach tightened. "I'll be extra careful. I won't get in any more trouble. Just watch."

"Yeah, Jack said the same thing. C'mon, let's go to the dining hall."

....

After supper Henry could not avoid Ruth. She cornered him and dragged him to the library. "Henry! What is wrong with you?"

"Nothing."

"You cheated in class today. That isn't 'nothing.'"

"I didn't know what else to do. I didn't hear what Miss Fannie had said the day before, so I didn't know the answers."

"That doesn't mean you should cheat!" In a softer tone, she said, "Okay. Just don't do it again."

"Yeah, sure." Henry walked back to the dorm. The sun had disappeared, leaving a thousand shimmering points of light against the night sky. He stopped and contemplated the magnitude of it all.

....

Tuesday, October 3, 1905

"Hurry up, or we won't be done before the girls come in to milk the cows!" Eddy fussed at Henry.

"Okay." Henry shut Jezebel's stall door and moved on to Daisy. Henry gave her hay and changed her water. He slipped out and bolted the door.

"We shouldn't have played with our dogs after breakfast. Frances and Elizabeth will be mad," Eddy said.

"It was your idea, Eddy." The boys picked up their pace and moved on to the horses. They finished with Apollo and Ajax and moved to Chance's stall. Out of the corner of his eye, Henry saw Jezebel's stall door open. Out lumbered the black cow, heading for the open barn door.

"Eddy! She's out! Jezebel's out!" Henry yelled, taking off after her. She sauntered out into the sunshine and turned to go behind the barn. "Help!"

Eddy yelled, "Don't run after her! Stop!" He slammed Chance's stall door shut and bolted it. Running to the entrance of the barn, he called after Henry, "Go get Mr. Dan! Now!"

Henry ran to the four-room shack and pounded on the door. "Mr. Dan! Mr. Dan!"

The door opened. "What's wrong?"

"Jezebel's out!" Henry pointed in her direction. Mr. Dan grabbed a rope from the shack's porch railing and went after her. She stopped to graze on a patch of grass. Approaching her slowly, he slipped the rope around her neck and led her back to her stall.

Henry bent over and put his hands on his knees, breathing hard. Mr. Dan walked up to him. "What happened?"

"We finished with her and were feeding and watering the horses when I saw her walk out of her stall. I don't know how she got out!"

"Did you bolt her door?"

"Yes, sir." Henry paused. "I'm pretty sure I did."

"She's not strong enough to get out of a locked door. You didn't bolt it." Henry's stomach did a flip-flop. Mr. Dan let the boys finish with Chance and Zippy, then instructed Henry to follow him to the schoolhouse. Eddy walked into the sunshine and watched Mr. Dan and Henry walk up the path. He kept his eyes on them until they reached the door.

Frances and Elizabeth eyed them as they continued to the barn. "Eddy, what happened?" Frances asked.

"Jezebel got out. Henry didn't bolt her door."

Frances gasped. "Oh, no!"

....

Mr. Dan had Henry sit on a chair outside Miss Gertrude's office while he told her what happened. Henry's head was swimming. Biting his fingernails, thoughts raced through his mind. *I can't believe I'm in trouble again. It wouldn't have happened if we weren't in such a rush.* Mr. Dan opened the door and motioned for him to come into Miss Gertrude's office. Henry stood and walked in. Mr. Dan left, shutting the door behind him, leaving Henry alone with her.

"Henry. You're in trouble for the second time in four days." Miss Gertrude frowned. "Your punishment today is five lashes and an hour and a half in the closet. I'm very disappointed in you, Henry. You've been at Pinehurst for six weeks now. Surely it's enough time to learn and understand all the rules."

Henry opened his mouth to object but then thought better of it. She stood and slipped the strap from around her neck. "Stand and put your hands on my desk."

18

The closet closed in on Henry. Tapping the back of his head against the wall, tears flowed down his face. He cried tears of anger, tears of frustration, tears of self-pity. He cried until there were no more tears to cry. He was consumed with an emptiness he'd never felt before. Thoughts of home flitted through his mind. The lump in his throat festered until he could no longer swallow. *I feel so sleepy.* Henry's head dropped, and he rested his chin on his chest. He closed his eyes.

Miss Gertrude opened the closet door at eleven-thirty. Vacant eyes met her gaze. "Let's go, Henry." Head down, he walked to the schoolhouse and followed Miss Gertrude to her office. "I want you to sit here until dinnertime." She poured a glass of water and set it in front of him. Henry took a seat. He stared at the glass but didn't acknowledge her. *Clang. Clang.* Miss Gertrude looked at Henry. "It's time for dinner." The first to arrive, she instructed him to take the seat closest to her.

A few minutes later, the students filled the hall. Henry heard them whisper and say his name. Apathy filled the void he'd felt earlier. Dinner was delivered and Henry took no notice. Ten minutes went by, and he had not picked up his fork. Miss Gertrude stood and helped Henry off the bench. She picked up his plate, and the two went into the kitchen. She pulled up a stool and had him sit at the spacious worktable. "Eat your dinner." She returned to the dining hall. At twelve-thirty she dismissed the children. Miss Gertrude returned to the kitchen to find Henry's food untouched. She frowned. "Let's go to my office."

Clang. Clang. Clang. Pursing her lips, Miss Gertrude observed the boy sitting across from her. "Henry?" Henry returned her gaze with blank eyes. "Henry?"

Miss Fannie knocked, opening the office door. "I wanted to check on Henry. How is he?"

"He has to go back to the dorm. He won't be able to do his job today. Would you please send Mr. Dan and Sammy to me?"

Miss Fannie frowned. "Yes, of course." She turned to leave, and stopped. Shifting her gaze, she faced her sister and hissed, "You've gone too far this time!" Miss Fannie left the office before Miss Gertrude had a chance to respond.

....

"Dan, I need you to help Jack and Will clean stalls, and Eddy to feed and water the livestock. Sammy will stay with Henry in their room."

"Yes, ma'am, Miss Gertrude," Mr. Dan said.

Sammy walked in. He looked at Henry and almost didn't recognize him. "You wanted to see me, Miss Gertrude?"

"Yes. I want you to take Henry back to the dorm and stay with him. Mr. Dan will do your job this afternoon."

Sammy leaned down and touched Henry's shoulder. "Hey, want to come with me?" Henry gave Sammy a slight nod. "Okay, let's go." Sammy helped him up and they left the office.

....

When they got to the room, Henry lay on his cot. He fell asleep and dreamed. He dreamed about the Fourth of July celebration he and his family went to only three months before. Henry was at the watermelon-eating contest table with Ruth. His father and Kate were watching, smiling and waving to them. Henry could feel the tension rising. He was determined to be the first one to finish. "On your mark. Get set. Go!" Henry's face dove into the melon, chomping as quickly as his mouth would allow. Melon juice dribbled down his chin. It went up his nose. It dripped on his shirt. He took the last bite and sat up. "I'm done!" He glanced around to see if there was anyone else sitting up. There wasn't. "I won!" Henry cheered. The judge pinned a blue ribbon on his shirt. The dream dwindled down to nothingness, leaving Henry with a warmth throughout his body. He stirred and woke. Henry opened his eyes and blinked. The warmth diminished and was replaced by sadness. He sniffed and sat up.

"How do you feel?"

Henry focused his eyes on Sammy. "Really tired and kind of sick."

"You've had a rough day. Want to talk about it?"

"Not right now. I want to go back to sleep." Henry lay back down and turned toward the wall.

Sammy grabbed his book and read.

Clang. Clang. Sammy got up and shook Henry's shoulder. "Hey, wake up. It's time for supper. C'mon."

"Mmm. Do I have to?" Henry mumbled.

"Yeah, you need to eat. Get up." Henry washed his face, and the boys walked to the dining hall without talking.

....

The aroma of ham and freshly baked bread stirred Henry's appetite. "I'm hungry," he whispered. They were the last to arrive, taking a seat at the end of the table. Henry shifted on the bench; he didn't like being stared at by the others. Miss Nellie walked in and began placing plates on the table. Miss Minnie served Sammy and Henry next. He couldn't wait to dig in. After supper Ruth grasped Henry's arm and pulled him in the direction of the library. He was dreading this.

"Henry! I'm worried about you. What happened? You weren't in class the whole day."

"Jezebel got out of her stall this morning. I got whipped and put in the closet for an hour and a half." Henry stared at Ruth with empty eyes.

"C'mon, tell me all of it."

Henry looked at Ruth, his expression blank. "After she whipped me, I don't know what happened. She put me in the closet, and I started to cry. I thought about a lot of different things. Then I stopped. I had no more tears. I wasn't sad, or mad, or happy, or anything. I was nothing. It's been like that all day."

"Maybe we should tell Father. He wouldn't want us to be here if he knew what was going on."

Henry looked into Ruth's eyes and spoke in a calm, flat voice. "Don't do it. The closet is horrible. She'd put you in it for hours." His voice dropped to a whisper. "Don't tell." He dropped his empty gaze. "Don't tell." Henry turned and walked away.

A tightness gripped Ruth's chest. What did she do to him? Ruth hung her head and cried.

....

Henry opened the door to his room. It was empty. He got his book and sat on his cot, propping himself against the wall. He opened the book and attempted to read. *We were in a hurry. That's why she got out.* His thoughts kept interrupting his reading. *But it was me who didn't check Jezebel's door. If I had . . .* Henry tried to drive the thoughts out of his mind. He had little success.

Sammy opened the door. "Hi. What are you doing?"

"Reading, but I can't concentrate." Henry closed his book. "Do we have time to play cards?"

"Sure, we can play."

....

Thursday, October 5, 1905

Miss Fannie reviewed multiplication with the older students, then gave them practice problems to complete. While they were working on their assignment, she taught a lesson on subtraction to the younger students. The room was quiet except for Miss Fannie's gentle voice and chalk marking on slates.

Clack! Pok, tok, pok, pok, tok. Sammy jumped out of his seat and went after the marble that fell out of his pocket. Miss Fannie noticed the commotion and glanced up in time to see Sammy sit down. She paused her lesson and walked to Sammy. "What was that noise, Sammy?" He opened his hand to expose his bright blue shooter marble. A look of disappointment flashed across Miss Fannie's face. She turned and walked to the front of the room and knocked on Miss Gertrude's door before stepping in. A few seconds later, both women came into the classroom. Miss Gertrude walked to Sammy's desk and held out her hand. Sammy dropped the marble into her palm.

"Come with me." They walked to her office, Sammy's head down. She pulled out a chair and he plopped down. Walking behind her desk, she kept her eyes on the boy. "You were in possession of a marble. Where are the rest of them?" Hesitating, Sammy pulled the cloth bag out of his front pocket and dropped them on the huge desk. "Where did you get these?"

"My parents gave them to me."

Miss Gertrude's frown deepened. "I'll make a note to speak to them to let them know such things are not allowed at Pinehurst. Who else knew about the marbles?" Sammy kept quiet. "Well?" Miss Gertrude spoke louder.

"Eddy and Henry."

"Did they play with the marbles?"

"Yes, ma'am."

"Since you've been cooperative, you'll receive three lashes instead of five. I do not want you to tell Eddy or Henry what you have told me. Do you understand?" Miss Gertrude's eyebrows pinched together.

"Yes, ma'am." After receiving the lashes, he returned to the classroom. Feeling the stares of the others, Sammy ignored them and picked up his slate. He continued with the arithmetic assignment.

....

Clang. Clang. Clang. The boys went to the barn to clean stalls. "So you got marbles?" Jack smiled.

"I did. Miss Gertrude took them." Sammy frowned.

"It's too bad. Marbles are fun."

When Henry and Eddy were leaving the barn, Mr. Dan walked up. "Eddy, I need to talk to you." Both boys stopped walking. "Henry, you go on and clean up."

"Yes, sir." *I wonder what that's about.* Henry went to the dorm.

"Miss Gertrude wants to talk to you." Mr. Dan and Eddy walked in silence to the schoolhouse. Eddy entered her office and she pointed at the chair across from her desk. He sat and stared at his folded hands.

"Did you know that Sammy had marbles?"

"Yes, ma'am."

"Why didn't you tell me? You know they are not allowed at Pinehurst."

"I didn't want Sammy to get in trouble."

"Did you play with the marbles?"

Eddy swallowed. "Yes, ma'am."

"In the future, you will tell me if you observe anything that shouldn't be here, correct?"

"Yes, ma'am."

"Who else knew about the marbles?"

"Um, Henry."

"Did he play with them, too?" Eddy nodded his head. "Because you've been truthful, I will not punish you this time. But be forewarned. If you conceal things from me again or take part in an activity which is forbidden, you will be punished. Please do not tell anyone about our conversation. Am I making myself clear?" Miss Gertrude's eyebrow shot up.

"Yes, ma'am."

....

Miss Gertrude dismissed the children from supper. She cornered Henry before he left the room. "Come with me." Henry followed her to her office. *What is going on?*

"Sit here." Miss Gertrude pulled out a chair. Henry sat down. His stomach fluttered. He noticed the bag on the desk.

"These are Sammy's marbles, as I'm sure you are aware. What I want to know, is, did you know about them?"

Henry, scared, wasn't sure what to say. *If I say yes, I'll get in trouble. If I say no, she might already know the truth.* He settled on being honest, "Yes, ma'am."

"Why didn't you tell me about them?"

"I was scared."

"Did you play with them?"

"No," Henry blurted out. Miss Gertrude scowled. In an instant, he knew he had said the wrong thing.

"You didn't play with them?" she paused. "You know it's not the truth, Henry. Would you like to try again?"

Henry squirmed. "Yes, I played with the marbles." His voice was barely audible.

"It appears you have trouble with remembering the rules. Do you know which rule you broke?"

"Yes, ma'am. I lied to you."

"Yes, you did. In addition to five lashes, you will go to the closet until bedtime." She checked the clock. "This will give you two and a half hours to think about the rules, and how you can make better choices. I want you to memorize the rules in order. You will repeat them to me when I come for you. I'm warning you, Henry. You must change your ways or you will face the full force of my wrath."

Henry flinched with each lash but did not cry out. The whippings weren't the worst part. Being shut in the closet was. He dreaded going into the small cubicle. He hated the darkness. He hated not being able to move around. He hated the loneliness which consumed him. *I hate that closet!*

"I will be back just before nine o'clock to let you out." She shut the door. The darkness crowded in on Henry. He tapped his forehead on the wall. *Stupid rules! I can't remember all of them, especially in order!* Henry wiped his tears and sniffed. His emotions all but abandoned him. *I don't care about her rules! She's the only one who does.* He continued to tap his head on the wall, losing all track of time.

….

Miss Gertrude opened the door. "Come out, Henry. Are you ready to tell me the rules?" He didn't respond. "Henry?" She took him by the arm and pulled him into the dimly lit hall. "Can you hear me?" Henry gazed at her with sunken eyes. "Do you think you can walk?"

"I don't know."

"Let's try. I want to put you into bed." Miss Gertrude helped him up and walked him to the staircase. "Here, try and go up the stairs." Henry took one riser at a time, holding on to the railing to steady himself. She got him in his room and onto his cot. He fell asleep almost immediately.

....

Friday, October 6, 1905

Rap, rap, rap. Sammy sat up and rubbed his face. "C'mon, time to wake up. Miss Gertrude walked you out of the dining hall after supper, and no one knew where you went. What happened?" Sammy asked.

Henry's memory was fuzzy. "She put me in the closet. I don't remember what happened afterward."

"You look terrible! Like you haven't slept for a week. We'll be late if we don't hurry. C'mon." Sammy helped Henry put on a fresh shirt, and the boys went to the bathroom to wash their faces. Last to arrive, they took a seat. Miss Minnie and Miss Nellie delivered breakfast. Henry stared at his plate.

Miss Gertrude and Miss Fannie, huddled together, spoke in whispers. "Henry did not take yesterday's punishment well. He seems to be suffering from a slight case of catatonia," Miss Gertrude said.

"We'll need to keep a close eye on him," Miss Fannie said. They walked back into the kitchen. Miss Fannie searched her heart for the right words to say to her sister. "Gertrude, you really need to tone down the punishment. They are just children, for God's sake."

Miss Gertrude raised her hand and *SMACK!* She slapped Miss Fannie across the face. "Are you questioning my methods? How dare you! You are the teacher. I run this school, and don't you forget it!" Taken aback, Miss Fannie's face flushed. She turned on her heel and walked out, cradling her cheek.

"Henry, you got to eat!" whispered Sammy. Henry stabbed at the scrambled eggs, his fork clinking against the plate. He nibbled at his breakfast. Upon dismissal, he went to the barn.

Henry stood at the feed bin holding the scoop, not moving. Eddy noticed, and asked, "What's wrong with you? Get the grain and feed the animals!" Henry didn't answer. Moving slowly, he filled the scoop with grain and dumped it in Daisy's bin.

....

Saturday, October 7, 1905

The boys walked out of the dorm and were greeted by a clear sky, the air somewhat cool. They were the first to arrive for breakfast. Jack came in, grumbling. "What's wrong with you?" Sammy asked.

"So much for a free afternoon. Mr. Dan said we have to pick corn today. It's gonna take all day. He'll be waiting for us by the barn as soon as we finish breakfast."

"That stinks. We go to class all week long, and then we got to work on Saturday, too." Sammy complained.

"That's not fair," Henry said.

"There's nothing fair about Pinehurst." Jack smirked.

....

Before dismissing the children from breakfast, Miss Gertrude told Jack, Sammy, and Will to stay behind. "Henry, I'd like you to stay too."

"You boys will assist Mr. Dan in the cornfield. He is waiting for you at the barn." The four boys walked to the barn, complaining the whole way.

Mr. Dan took the boys to the cornfield and demonstrated how to strip the husks from the corn and yank the cob from the stalk. "I'll have a wagon out here. When you pull the ear off the stalk, throw it in the back. We will start on the far side," Mr. Dan said, then went to the barn to get the work wagon. Mr. Dan drove Zippy into the cornfield, between two rows of corn plants. He pointed to Jack and Henry. "Y'all come over to this side of the wagon. We'll start out slow, but you'll need to speed up. Find a spot and get goin'."

Henry took an ear of corn, ripped the husk off, and snapped it off the stalk. He threw it into the wagon. He grabbed another and repeated the process. The more he worked, the more proficient he became. Mr. Dan edged the wagon further into the cornfield and they picked up their pace. *This isn't so bad.* Henry yanked another shucked ear off the stalk and tossed it in the wagon.

After two hours of working, Mr. Dan shouted, "Break time!" He ladled out water from a bucket and let the boys drink. The sun rose higher in the sky, and the temperature climbed as they continued to work.

Henry wiped the sweat from his brow. "It's getting hot out here," he said.

"It'll be worse this afternoon," Jack said, tossing an ear onto the growing pile of corn.

At quarter till noon, Mr. Dan dismissed them to the dorm to get cleaned up for dinner. The first to arrive in the dining hall, Henry and Sammy plopped down on the bench. "That sure is hard work. It was easy at first, then my arms started getting tired," Henry complained.

"Yeah, mine, too."

19

By midafternoon, Henry was spent. His arms felt like lead weights. Red splotches had popped up all over his forearms. Miserable, Henry wiped his brow to keep the sweat from running into his eyes. He stared out at the sea of corn waving in the breeze. At three-thirty, Mr. Dan dismissed Sammy, Will, and Jack to clean the stalls. He looked to Henry. "Since you don't need to feed the animals until four o'clock, we'll keep working." Henry groaned. "Miss Gertrude says we have to finish this row." Henry snapped a husked ear off and tossed it in the wagon. Thirty minutes passed. "Okay, Henry. I'll bring in the livestock. You go on over to the barn."

....

Henry and Eddy sat in the aisle with their backs against the huge door while they waited for the animals to come in. "How'd you get so lucky?" Eddy asked.

"What do you mean?"

"Picking corn. Why'd you have to?"

"I don't know. I think Miss Gertrude doesn't like me because I've been in trouble a lot."

"Maybe. She was like that with Jack last year."

"She was?"

"Yeah. Jack's been here a long time. Says she does it every year— singles out one kid and picks on him."

Henry pondered Eddy's words. *She's the reason I've been getting in trouble! Miss Gertrude is picking on me!*

Henry went to the dorm to wash up. His arms were itching like crazy, but it hurt to scratch them. He examined his arms more closely. What he thought were just bumps were dozens of tiny blisters. He went to his room and found Sammy playing solitaire. Henry held out his arms. "Look at these red bumps, Sammy."

"Did you have it before picking the corn?"

"No, after I started."

"I bet it's from the corn. I remember last year, this kid named Andy got it real bad. His arms were red for two weeks. But yours doesn't seem too bad. You should ask Miss Minnie for help."

....

Henry walked to the schoolhouse and knocked on the kitchen door. Miss Minnie opened the door. "What is it?"

"My arms hurt. I've got some kind of rash. I got it from picking corn."

"Let's take a look." Henry showed her his arms. "Yes, it's red corn rash, all right." Pointing, she said, "Sit over there." Miss Minnie took a jar of oatmeal off the shelf and dumped it in a pan, then filled it with water. "Here, soak your arms in this for twenty minutes or so. Don't scratch them."

Miss Gertrude entered through the swinging door. "What have we here, Miss Minnie?" she asked, her malcontented gaze settling on Henry.

"Henry's got red corn rash. He's soaking his arms in oatmeal."

"Let me see your arms, Henry." She inspected them and frowned. "You'll need to soak them for a while longer, and we may need to put compresses on them, too."

"Yes, ma'am." Henry observed the rash. The red had subsided some and was now bright pink. The bell rang twice. Miss Minnie and Miss Nellie got the plates ready and began serving them. Miss Minnie placed a plate of ham, mashed sweet potatoes, and a biscuit next to Henry. Miss Minnie and Miss Nellie put the cooking pots and pans in the deep double sink and began washing them. They talked in hushed voices while they worked. Henry strained his ears to hear what they were saying.

"According to Gertrude, we have 'the' troublemaker with us." Miss Minnie handed a pot to Miss Nellie.

"He seems like a nice boy. I wouldn't think he's the bad one in the bunch," Miss Nellie said.

"What do you mean? He's gotten in trouble five times in as many weeks."

"I know, but you didn't see him yesterday morning. Poor thing stared at his food when I put it in front of him. Miss Gertrude really gave it to him Thursday evening. I think it made Miss Fannie upset."

"Gertrude does what has to be done around here. These children need discipline to keep things running smoothly." Miss Minnie picked up a dishtowel and dried a pot, then walked over to Henry. "Let's take another look." He took his arms out of the pan and showed them to her. "We'll dry them off, and I'll give you compresses to put on them." She took a bottle off the shelf and soaked two dishrags in apple cider vinegar. "Here, put these on your arms." Henry sat at the small table with his arms outstretched, the smelly compresses in place, his eyes watering from the strong odor. After thirty minutes, she removed them. "They appear to be better. How do they feel? Do they still itch?"

"A little bit."

"All right. Don't scratch them. If you do, it will make it worse."

"Yes, ma'am." Henry left and went to his room.

....

Sunday, October 8, 1905

Leaving breakfast, Ruth caught up to Henry. "Where were you at suppertime yesterday?"

"I was in the kitchen soaking my arms." Henry showed her his forearms.

"Boy, they sure look like they hurt."

"They don't hurt much, but they sure are itchy. They're better today than yesterday, but I don't know what I'll tell Father. I can't tell him I got the rash while picking corn."

"You're right. I don't think there is a way to hide it from him. You may need to fib to him."

"I can't lie to Father!"

"I know. But consider the consequences—if you tell him the truth, you'll be punished again. Probably worse than before."

"What should I say?"

"You can tell him you took Buster out in the woods yesterday and got into poison ivy or poison oak."

"I guess I can. I just hate lying to him."

····

Henry opened the dorm door. "Hey, Sammy. Do you think I'd be in trouble if Miss Gertrude found out I told my father I had to pick corn yesterday?"

"You got to ask me? Of course you'd get in trouble. Why would you even consider telling him?"

"He'll see my arms." Henry held out his arms.

"Oh yeah, you got that rash. It doesn't seem too bad today."

"Yeah, but he'll still notice it. Ruth said I should fib to him. Say it's poison ivy or poison oak. I don't want to lie to him."

"You might need to. If you tell him the truth, and he says somethin' to Miss Gertrude, she will deny it. She'll tell your father you made it up. Then you'll get in bad trouble."

"I guess I need to fib. I just don't want to."

"Yeah, but you don't have much of a choice."

Henry opened his book: Part VI, "In the Enemy's Camp." He read a few minutes until the bell rang.

····

Once everyone was seated, Miss Gertrude and the children recited the Lord's Prayer. When the room was silent, she continued, "Today's lesson is on temptation. The word "temptation" comes from the word "tempt." To tempt means to be enticed to do something which is unwise, wrong, or immoral." Miss Gertrude gave a long, rambling sermon on how the flesh is weak and is easily tempted to do wrong. "You may be tempted to break a rule or your silence. You must pray to God to lead you from the temptation and keep you from doing evil." Miss Gertrude directed the children's attention to the blackboard. "Our hymn today is 'The Unchanging Word.'"[1]

....

Henry saw Jack walking to the barn. "Hey, Jack! Wait up."

"Hi. Another great Bible lesson, huh?" Jack said.

"Yeah." Henry paused. "The other day, Sammy and I were talking, and I told him Miss Gertrude said, 'I'm keeping my eye on you,' to me. He said she told you the same thing. Did she? What happened?"

"Yeah, she did. I kept getting in trouble, no matter how careful I was. It took me a while to realize what she was doing. She gave me stuff that would either be too hard for me to do, or be able to finish in time, making me late to the dining hall."

"I overheard Miss Minnie say I was 'the' troublemaker."

"Oh, boy. Miss Gertrude's got you singled out. She'll use you as an example for the other kids, so they'll be too scared to break a rule."

The color drained from Henry's face. "What am I supposed to do?"

"You've got to do your best and work fast. As long as there are no grownups around, I can help you do the extra chores."

"You'd do that for me?"

"Yeah, you're a nice kid. I don't want you to get in any more trouble."

"Thanks, Jack." Henry didn't know he would be getting Jack's help later that day.

....

1. Charles W. Naylor, "The Unchanging Word," 1900.

Henry and Ruth saw the chestnut gelding plodding up the drive. "Here they come!" Ruth pointed to the end of the driveway. They jumped off the porch and met the carriage as it rolled to a stop. After hugs and small talk, Ruth said, "We've been busy learning a lot about plants. Want to see our vegetables in the garden?"

"Show us the way," Herman said.

"Here are my tomatoes," Henry said. "They're doing great."

"Yes, they are." Kate smiled. "You're taking good care of them."

"Look here." Henry cradled the small fruit in his hand. "It's growing big!"

"It sure is," Herman said. "It's going to be gigantic!"

Henry gaped at his father. "Probably the biggest tomato ever!"

Herman laughed. "So, Ruthie, show us your plot."

Ruthie walked to another section of the garden and pointed to broccoli plants. "Here's mine. They are growing big, too."

"They certainly are. You two are regular farmers now!" Herman winked at Ruth. "Why don't we sit at the picnic tables and chat? Henry, we can play catch, if you'd like."

Herman and Henry threw the ball back and forth while Kate and Ruth sat in the shade at one of the picnic tables, talking. "Are things any easier for you, Ruth? I mean about being away from home?" Kate asked.

"Sort of. A day doesn't go by that I don't think of Father and you. We both miss being at home. We're really looking forward to Christmastime."

"We miss you also. Your Father talks about you two all the time."

"Whew! Did you see that throw? I think Henry's ready to join the big leagues!" Herman said, walking up to the table. He sat down and wiped his brow. Henry sat next to his father, a smile spreading across his face.

Herman noticed Henry's arms. "Is that a rash?"

Henry looked at them, then his father. "Um, yes, sir. I, uh, got it when I was out in the woods with Buster yesterday. He went under a bush, and I had to pull him out. I guess I got into poison ivy or something." He felt a knot building in his stomach. "Miss Minnie had me soak them, then put some smelly rags on them. It helped make them feel better."

Herman glanced at Kate. "She probably used apple cider vinegar," she said. Herman nodded.

"Be careful what you get into out there, okay?"

"Yes, sir." Feeling guilty for lying, Henry broke out into a light sweat. Maybe now's a good time to tell Father about all the extra work and the punishment. Henry's demeanor changed, garnering Herman's attention.

"Henry, what's wrong?"

"Uh, nothing Father." His heart rate sped up. *I'm afraid to tell him!* "I just got a little hot."

"You sure?"

Henry nodded, a blank expression crossing his face. The family settled into a conversation about home and Christmastime, enjoying their visit. They were disappointed when their time together came to a close.

Herman and Kate returned to the carriage, waving goodbye. They boarded the wagon and Hercules schlepped down the drive. "Henry's response about the rash was a bit off. Like he wasn't sure what he was doing when he got it," Herman said, turning north onto the main road. "His behavior was off after that. Did you notice?"

"Yes, I did. I'm sure it's nothing. You know how kids can be; he probably just misses being at home."

"I hope you're right."

"He's a good boy, Herman. I'm sure everything is fine."

....

After his father and Kate departed, Henry went to his room and got his book. He went to the library and settled into one of the overstuffed chairs. Henry opened the book to chapter twenty-nine: "The Black

Spot Again." Captivated by the story, he didn't notice Miss Gertrude enter the room.

"Hello, Henry." The sound of her voice startled him and his book clattered to the floor. He scrambled to pick it up.

"Hello, Miss Gertrude." Henry's heart thumped in his chest.

"I have to interrupt your reading and give you a job to do before feeding the livestock this afternoon. The water troughs in the stalls need to be scrubbed. Work quickly so you'll be finished before Mr. Dan brings the animals in the barn. Here's the brush."

"Yes, ma'am." Taking the brush from her, he checked the time: three-thirty. Jack should be in the barn cleaning stalls. Henry scooted to the barn, brush in hand.

He found Jack in Daisy's stall. "Hey, Jack. Miss Gertrude told me I need to scrub out all the water troughs before Mr. Dan lets the animals in the barn."

"She's starting already." Jack rolled his eyes. "Start in here, I'm almost done." Five minutes later, Jack hung the pitchfork on the wall and got another brush. "She'll come in and check all of them to make sure you did it right. Let me show you how I do it." Jack took the brush and scrubbed, showing Henry how to get the most grime out with the least effort in the shortest amount of time. "Okay, this one is done. You finish the cows' troughs, and I'll do the horses'."

Henry's eyes brightened. "Thanks, Jack." He went to Cookie's stall next and scrubbed the trough the way Jack showed him. Henry worked fast and was finishing up in Jezebel's stall when Jack walked in. "Whew! Thanks for helping me, Jack. I couldn't have done it without you."

"Sure. That's what friends are for." He winked at Henry. "The horses' troughs are clean, so you're all set. See you later."

"Okay, bye." *She won't get me this time!*

....

"Hi, Henry. You're here early," Eddy said.

"Yeah. Miss Gertrude gave me an extra job to do—scrubbing the water troughs. Just finished them." Mr. Dan opened the rear doors, and moments later the livestock entered and went into their stalls.

When they were about to leave, Miss Gertrude walked in. "Hello, boys. Henry, did you finish scrubbing the troughs?"

"Yes, ma'am."

"Let's take a look." She went to each stall, inspecting the troughs, searching for dirty areas. Miss Gertrude found none and frowned. "It appears you've done the job adequately. Be on time for supper."

"Yes, ma'am."

"C'mon, let's go clean up," Eddy said.

"You go ahead. I'll check the latches one more time," Henry said. He pulled on each of the horse's doors. All secure. He crossed the dusty aisle and walked down the other side. Henry pulled on Daisy's door: good. He continued. Good. Good. He got to Cookie's and pulled. *Creeeeaak.* His stomach rolled. Henry slammed the door shut and bolted the latch. His hand flew to his mouth and cupped it in disbelief. *I bolted it!* Henry's eyes widened. *She did it! She did it and was going to blame me for leaving it unlatched!* Henry's heart raced.

After supper, Henry sought out Jack. He told him what had happened in the barn. "Do you think she did it on purpose? To blame me?"

Jack smirked and nodded. "Yeah, that was her plan. She did that kind of stuff to me, too. But you were smart! You checked the latches. Keep on your toes and double-check everything."

"Okay, thanks."

....

"Hi," Henry said, opening the door.

"Where were you?" Sammy asked.

"I was reading in the library and talking to Jack.

"So why were you scrubbing the water troughs today?"

Henry told him what Miss Gertrude did, and what Jack had said about it. "Jack knows her better than anyone. Listen to what he says. I can help you, too, you know." Sammy's lip curled up.

"You will? Thanks!"

"We ought to let Eddy in on this, too. With the four of us working together, you won't be getting in trouble. C'mon, let's go wash up and get ready for bed."

....

Tuesday, October 10, 1905

Henry scanned the pack of dogs, trying to find Buster. A knot grew in his stomach. *I've got to find him!* Henry walked around and among the dogs calling out Buster's name.

"What's wrong?" Jack said, walking up to Henry.

"I can't find Buster. He's not here!"

"Did you look around for him?"

"Not yet!"

Sammy walked up. "What's going on?"

"Can't find Buster. Let's split up and try to find him." Pointing to Sammy, Jack said, "You go to the cornfield. Henry, start in the barn. I'll check behind the barn. Hey, Eddy, come here!"

"Yeah?"

"Help us find Buster. Check the chicken coop and pig sty."

"Yeah, okay," said Eddy.

The boys split up and searched for the dog. Sammy and Eddy got finished and went to the barn to help Henry. They checked each stall, near the grain bins, and up in the hayloft. No sign of Buster. "What am I going to do?" Henry whimpered.

Yip, yip, yap. Henry swung around to find Buster running into the barn with Jack close behind.

"Buster! Where were you?" Henry looked at Jack. "Where did you find him?"

"You won't believe it. He was locked in one of the sheds." Jack shook his head.

20

"How did he get locked . . ." Henry's eyes grew round. "You mean, she did it?" His stomach rolled.

"Yeah, somebody did. I doubt if it was Mr. Dan or Mr. John," Jack said. "C'mon, let's go feed 'em."

Thoughts swirled in Henry's head as he fed Buster. *She wants me to get in trouble! She's doing things so she can punish me.* Miss Gertrude opened the back door and scanned the pack of dogs. Her gaze stopped on Buster, and her frown deepened. Glaring at Henry, her eyes narrowed. Placing the scoop back in the bin, Henry smiled at her. "Good morning, Miss Gertrude." She huffed, turned, and walked back inside, slamming the door.

"Boy, Henry. Did you see her face? She sure was mad," Jack said, laughing.

"I'll say," added Sammy.

"I probably shouldn't have said 'good morning' to her."

Jack laughed. "I thought it was great. She didn't know what to say after that!"

....

After breakfast Jack went to the barn to find Henry and Eddy feeding the animals. "Hey, Henry. After what happened this morning, there's no doubt she's got it in for you. You can't let her win. We can't let her win."

"What do you mean, 'can't let her win?'"

"Did you forget to latch the stall door? Were you unable to find Buster? Was either of those your fault? No. This is like a game to her. A game she wants to win, no matter what. I learned that the hard way. It took me a long time to figure it out."

Henry went pale. "What else will she do?"

"I don't know. She'll think of something, though. That's why you have to be extra careful. And why we need to stick together so you don't get in trouble."

....

Henry sat at his desk and only half-listened to Miss Fannie's lecture on conjugating verbs. His thoughts were on what happened earlier. A chill worked its way down his back. *"We can't let her win," Jack said. I almost got in trouble twice for things I didn't do!* Henry forced himself to quiet his thoughts and turned his attention to the grammar lesson.

....

Miss Fannie took the children outside for a midafternoon break. While the boys played a game of dodgeball, Ruth and Lorene played cat's cradle at one of the tables. Ruth noticed that Grace was sitting under an oak tree by herself. "Hi, Grace. How are you?" Ruth asked, sitting next to her. Grace looked at Ruth and did not respond at first.

"I didn't mean for the chick to get out," Grace whispered, staring straight ahead.

Ruth tilted her head slightly and pursed her lips. "I know, Grace. It was an accident. Are you doing better?"

"Better? Better than what?" Grace said, not seeming to understand.

Ruth gently shook her head. "Nothing, Grace. It's okay." She gave Grace a quick hug, said goodbye, and went back over to Lorene. "Grace is still upset about the chick. She doesn't seem to know that it happened weeks ago." Ruth stood and went to where Miss Fannie was standing. "Miss Fannie, um, Grace isn't herself. She's still upset about the chick."

"Yes, I noticed that as well. I will have to speak to her again." Miss Fannie was at a loss. Surely Grace should be getting past the incident.

....

Clang. Clang. Clang. Miss Fannie dismissed the students. Realizing he had missed half of the grammar lesson, Henry didn't understand how to conjugate some verbs. Before he could ask for help, the teacher walked into Miss Gertrude's office. He waited by the door for Miss Fannie to come out. Henry heard them talking, and it sounded like Miss Gertrude was getting mad. He listened more intently.

"Fannie, I said I need your help. We've got to have a situation where he'll break a rule. I can't do it this time. Have him miss an assignment or catch him copying someone's slate again. Or trip him up in some other way."

"I will not do your dirty work, Gertrude! I've turned a blind eye to your behavior toward the children for too long. I will not be a part of your sick little game." Henry heard this and quietly scooted back to his desk and sat down, his heart racing.

"You will not speak to me that way!" Miss Gertrude reached for the leather strap. The door to Miss Gertrude's office door flew open, and Miss Fannie stormed out. Miss Gertrude, seething, laid eyes on Henry and stopped short of walking into the classroom. She turned and went back to her office, slamming the door behind her.

"Oh, Henry! I didn't realize you were still here. Is there something you need?" Miss Fannie said, her face still flushed with anger.

"Yes, Ma'am, I need help with today's grammar lesson."

"Very well." She called Henry to the front of the room, and using the blackboard, went through a brief lesson on verb conjugation. "Now do you understand?"

"Yes, I think so."

Ting. Ting. Ting. Ting. He glanced at the clock and jumped up. "Thanks, Miss Fannie. I've got to do my job now." Henry took a step toward the door and hesitated. He turned back and gave her a hug.

....

"Where were you? I didn't think you were coming," Eddy said.

"I was talking to Miss Fannie. I'll fetch the hay." Henry scaled the ladder and threw down the pads of hay. When they were done, Henry offered to check the latches. Eddy passed Jack on the way out.

179

"Hi, Henry, what's going on?" Jack said.

"Hi. I'm checking the latches. I overheard Miss Gertrude tell Miss Fannie she needed help to 'trip him up.' I know she was talking about me."

"What did Miss Fannie say?"

"She said she wouldn't do her dirty work for her. Miss Gertrude was mad."

"So, now she's trying to get help. Sounds like Miss Fannie won't do it. But you still need to be careful. And don't forget to ask us for help."

"Thanks, Jack. It means a lot to me."

Jack smiled. "You're like my brother, and brothers have to stick together. See you around."

"'Bye, Jack." Henry turned his attention back to checking the latches.

....

Saturday, October 14, 1905

Before dismissing the children from breakfast, Miss Gertrude announced, "Today you will assist Mr. John and Mr. Dan in the fields planting seeds. Meet behind the schoolhouse at eight-thirty. You will be given a ten-minute warning."

The children groaned in response. "Not again," Eddy said, rolling his eyes.

"It's not fair. She's got us working almost every Saturday!" Henry complained. The boys left the dining hall and went to feed the horses and cows.

After working most of the day in the sun, the children were exhausted. "I'm tired and my back hurts," Sammy said.

"Yeah, mine does, too," Jack said. "Now we get to go clean stalls! Lucky us."

....

Monday, October 16, 1905

Dan checked his watch: five-fifty. "John," he called out. "I'm going over to check on Zippy. I'll be back in a few minutes to finish cooking the corn." Dan noticed Zippy was limping earlier when he brought the animals in from the pasture. He led him out of the stall and into the aisle. After a few steps, he determined Zippy was favoring his left rear leg. "Okay, boy. Let's take a look." He lifted the horse's leg and felt around the inside of his shoe. He discovered a stone lodged between the inner edge of his hoof and the shoe. "No wonder you were limping." Dan got the rasp. With its pointed end, he popped out the stone. He led the horse back to his stall and latched the door. *Might as well check all the latches while I'm out here.* He walked down the aisle pulling on each stall door. He headed back to the shack to finish cooking supper.

When Dan was getting ready to turn in, he heard the horses whinnying. *Bam!* One of the horses kicked the side of his stall. *Bam!* "What's got them so stirred up?" He grabbed his hat and walked over to the barn. Once inside, he raised the lantern above his head. Letting his eyes adjust, he noticed the aisle was empty and the front door was partially open. "What the . . . ?" Mr. Dan slid it shut. Raising the lantern again, he looked into each stall. Zippy was pacing, obviously spooked. "What's got into you, boy?" Dan lowered the light and reached his arm in to stroke Zippy's head. "It's okay, boy. Nothin' going on here." The horse, comforted by Dan's touch, settled down. Out of habit, he walked down the row of stalls and tugged on each door. He almost stumbled when Chance's door opened. "What . . . ?" He quickly shut and bolted it. "Now I know I checked them before supper!" His gaze went to the front door again and back to Chance's stall. "Who in tarnation would do something like this?"

....

Tuesday, October 17,1905

After breakfast Henry walked to the barn. The chill in the air was refreshing. He pulled on the heavy barn door and inched it open. He was surprised Mr. Dan was standing by Zippy in the middle of the aisle. "Hi, Mr. Dan."

"Morning, Henry."

"Is something wrong with Zippy?"

"One of his hooves is sore. Just checking it." Mr. Dan untied the horse and led him back to his stall. "I'll be back in a few minutes." He walked out and closed the back doors.

"You're here early," Eddy said.

"Yeah. Thought I'd start early, but I didn't. I was talking to Mr. Dan. I guess Zippy hurt one of his hooves."

"The sooner we get done, the better." The boys got finished in record time. Henry offered to check the latches and Eddy left to go back to the dorm.

"All of them secure?" The sound of Mr. Dan's voice startled Henry.

"Yes, sir." Henry nodded.

"I want you to come with me."

Henry swallowed. "Where are we going?"

"To talk to Miss Gertrude."

Henry's stomach rolled. *Why do I have to see her?*

Mr. Dan saw Henry's expression. "Don't worry, kid. You ain't got nothin' to be afraid of."

Henry followed Mr. Dan and stared at the ground in front of him, his heartbeat thumping with each step. *If I don't have anything to be afraid of, then why do I have to go to Miss Gertrude?*

Mr. Dan knocked on the office door. "Come in," said the gravelly voice.

Miss Gertrude looked up from her paperwork, and a smile cracked her face. "Well, Mr. Dan. What do have we here?" Her gaze settled on Henry.

"We've got a problem, Miss Gertrude. I believe someone is trying to get Henry in trouble. I checked all the stall latches while Henry was at supper, and they were all secure. Before I turned in for the night, one of the horses was making a ruckus. When I got there, the front door was partially open, and Chance's door was unlatched! Someone went into the barn after I checked them and purposely opened the latch."

21

Miss Gertrude's fractured smile turned into a deep frown. She stared at Mr. Dan; her eyes bulging. "Well, Mr. Dan. I . . ."

"You did it! You want me to get in trouble so you can punish me!" Henry slapped his hand across his mouth and trembled, his heart pounding.

Miss Gertrude's face flushed as she clenched her jaw. "What did you say?"

A surge of energy and confidence coursed through Henry—something he had never felt before. He looked at her, his eyes dilated and wild. "I said you unlatched the door so I would be blamed and be in trouble. You want to punish me!"

"How dare you! How dare you disrespect me! You'll pay dearly for your smart mouth!" Mr. Dan put his arm around Henry and pulled him closer. Sounding like a demon, Miss Gertrude hissed, "Mr. Dan, I want you to leave now." Her voice turned Henry's blood to ice.

Mr. Dan hesitated. He didn't want to leave Henry. "Miss Gertrude, with all due respect, I think I'll stay."

Glaring at Mr. Dan with protruding eyes, Miss Gertrude pulled the strap from her neck. Henry walked to her desk and placed his hands on the edge and leaned over, waiting for the impending pain.

"Your punishment is ten lashes and three and a half hours in the closet!" Spittle flew from her lips, her mouth stretching into a snarl. Without missing a beat, she whacked Henry with the strap.

Smack! "Mmmppfff." *Smack!* "Mmmppfff." She continued hitting him, a little harder each time. Henry clamped his jaw and squeezed his lips together. *I will not cry out!* When she was done, Miss Gertrude returned the strap to her neck. Henry stood and faced her with a glimmer in his eyes. *You won't win!*

Miss Gertrude pulled him by the ear and led him out of the schoolhouse and into the dormitory. "You will stay here until dinner time!" She slammed the closet door and stomped out.

Henry's head was spinning. What just happened? He closed his eyes and tried to calm his pounding heart. His weak legs wouldn't hold him any longer. He slid down the wall, his knees touching his chest. Sleepy, he closed his eyes, the knot in his stomach softening.

Henry didn't know how much time had passed when he awoke. His legs were cramping, his neck stiff. He felt for the doorknob and was surprised it turned. Henry opened the door and with the extra room, he was able to stand. The fresh air was invigorating, and he inhaled deeply. The drowsiness vanished and he was acutely aware of his surroundings. All the times he got in trouble at home and at Pinehurst crowded his thoughts. Henry glanced around, then stepped back into the closet and shut the door. He stretched his back and stood up straight, and the stress flowed out of his body like water from a broken dam. He felt as though the lightness in his chest would lift him off the floor. He smiled. *Everything will be all right.*

At eleven-forty, Miss Gertrude opened the closet door. Expecting a cowering, defeated soul, she instead found a boy who was calm and sanguine. She took a step back and scowled. "I want you to go wash up and change for dinner. Be on time!"

"Yes, ma'am." Henry hopped upstairs and washed up. He changed his clothes and went to the dining hall. Henry sat next to Jack and smiled.

"What are you so happy about? I heard you got in trouble," Jack said.

"I did."

"Well? You plan on telling me why you're smiling, or do I have to pull it out of you?"

"I'll tell you this afternoon in the barn."

"Okay, Jack said, shrugging his shoulders.

....

After class, the older boys went to clean stalls. Henry showed up fifteen minutes later. "Hi, boys."

Jack nodded to Henry, then looked at Sammy with a raised eyebrow. Sammy shrugged. "Hey, Will, why don't you go on back to the dorm. Me and Sammy got this," Jack said.

"Yeah? It sure is nice of you."

"Yeah, go on." Jack waited until Will walked out. He turned to Henry. "So what happened? You got punished, and you're smiling. That doesn't make any sense!"

Henry told them Mr. Dan had taken him to Miss Gertrude's office and he was afraid he was in trouble. "Yeah, and Mr. Dan said, 'You ain't got nothin' to be afraid of.' I didn't know what he meant. When we got to her office, he told her he thought someone was trying to get me in trouble, since Chance's door was unlatched after he had checked it. You should've seen her face. I've never seen her so mad!" Eddy walked up and listened in. "I don't know why I did it, but I said, 'You're the one who did it! You wanted me to get in trouble.' Then something happened inside me. Something snapped. She asked me to repeat what I said, so I did. Miss Gertrude blew her top. She hit me ten times with the strap, then put me in the closet 'til dinnertime."

Jack, Sammy, and Eddy stared at him in disbelief. "Aw, c'mon, Henry. You expect us to believe that?" Sammy asked.

"It did happen! Mr. Dan was there. You can ask him!"

"Ask him what?" Mr. Dan's baritone voice startled the boys.

"Um, w-what happened this morning."

"Henry, you were quite the rebel. You're the first one to stand up to her. I thought I'd seen everything, but you really surprised me. How are you doing now?" Mr. Dan asked, patting Henry on the shoulder.

"I'm okay. I was telling them something changed inside me. I'm not afraid of her anymore," Henry said with his newfound confidence.

"Wow, I can't believe you did it!" Jack said.

"Yeah, me, too," Sammy added.

"I wish I had guts like you," Eddy said.

"You're a smart boy, Henry. But don't let your guard down. She may back down, or she may not. Be careful." Mr. Dan looked at Henry with admiration. "Okay, boys, you have ten minutes to finish with the stalls. I'll bring the livestock into the barn in just a bit."

....

"You and I are going to the library after supper!" Ruth said to Henry, walking around the massive table. She took a seat on the bench, staring at her brother.

Miss Gertrude sat at the head of the table. "Let us pray." The children bowed their heads while she gave thanks. Henry felt her eyes burning into him as he took a bite of supper. He glanced up at her and smiled. Her expression went from evil to rattled. Miss Gertrude ate her supper without looking at him again. Henry gazed out the window. Contented, he relaxed, closed his eyes, and took in a deep breath.

After supper, Ruth confronted Henry. "Come with me." She pulled him into the library. Sitting across from him with her arms folded on the table, she said, "Would you mind telling me what's going on? I heard you got in trouble this morning. Yet here you are, acting as though everything is fine. Have you lost your mind?"

Henry smiled. "No, I'm okay." He started at the beginning and told Ruth everything. She stared at him, finding it hard to believe all that he told her. Ruth raised her eyebrows. "Come on, Henry."

"Like I said, something burst inside me. I don't know what it was or why it happened. It felt like I was seeing the whole world differently. It's hard to explain. Not only did I mouth off to her, all the times I ever got in trouble flashed through my mind. It was always my fault, Ruth! I know that now. I don't know why it took me so long to get it. I wasn't punished because Kate didn't like me, or because she was picking on me. I was punished for doing something wrong! I broke the rules here. That's why I was punished!" Henry sat back and relaxed. "Now that I know why I was punished, I never have to be punished again. It's always been my choice!"

Gazing at Henry in astonishment, Ruth saw the sparkle in his eyes—a sparkle she hadn't seen since their mother died. Placing her palm on her chest, Ruth reached out and touched Henry's arm. She shook her head, searching for the right words. "Henry, I am so proud of you! You're so brave." Her eyes watered as she squeezed his arm. "Father would be proud of you, too." She noticed the sheen on his face. "You're sweaty. You okay?"

"I think so. I'm tired, though."

....

Henry lay in bed replaying the day's events in his mind. *I can't believe I said she did it!* His adrenaline rush had worn off, and fear of reprisal crept into his mind. Drenched in sweat, he took his nightshirt off and threw it on the floor. A restless sleep overtook his exhausted body and mind.

....

Wednesday, October 18, 1905

Sammy sat on the edge of his cot. "C'mon, it's time to wake up." Henry didn't move. "I said time to get up."

"Hmmm. I don't feel so good."

"What's the matter?"

"My head hurts real bad, and I'm sweaty."

"Go wash your face. It might make you feel better," Sammy said. Henry went to the bathroom and splashed cool water on his sweaty face. He felt no better.

Miss Minnie and Miss Nellie served scrambled eggs and bacon, one of Henry's favorites. *Glurp!* "I feel like throwing up!" Henry whispered to Sammy. "I can't eat."

"Yeah, you look sick. After breakfast I'll help Eddy feed and water the animals and you ask Miss Minnie if she can help you."

"Okay." Henry mushed the eggs around on his plate and didn't take a bite. Miss Gertrude dismissed the children and left to go to her office. Slow to get up, Henry was the last to stand. Miss Nellie came in to take the empty plates.

"Why, you haven't touched your food! What's the matter, Henry?"

187

"I feel sick."

"Come to the kitchen with me. Miss Minnie will know what to do," Miss Nellie said in a comforting voice.

"What's wrong with him?" Miss Minnie asked, somewhat perturbed, as Miss Nellie and Henry entered the kitchen.

"He says he doesn't feel well, and he didn't touch his food."

"Okay, Henry. What is it?"

"My head hurts really bad, and I feel like I'm going to throw up."

Miss Minnie placed her palm on his forehead. "Hm. You have a slight fever and you're sweating, too. How long have you felt like this?"

"Last night I was sweaty, and my head hurt. I felt like throwing up when I smelled breakfast."

"Stay here. I'll be right back." Minnie went to the classroom and found Fannie working on the day's lesson. "Fannie, Henry is sick. I don't think he should come to class today."

"What's wrong?" Fannie said, putting her pen down.

"He's got a bad headache, he's sweaty, and has nausea. He doesn't appear well at all. I think he should rest under supervision. I'll take him to our living quarters and get Nellie to keep an eye on him."

"Yes, good idea. If there's anything I can do, please let me know."

....

Miss Nellie walked Henry to the downstairs of the dormitory and led him to a sofa in the Anhorns' parlor. "I want you to lie here, Henry. I'll get a cool cloth for your forehead and bring you a glass of water. Can I get you anything?"

Henry lay on the sofa, curled up on his side. "Can I have my quilt?" Henry whispered.

"Yes, I'll get it for you. I'll be right back." She returned, placing the quilt over Henry. Miss Nellie put the cloth on his head and wiped his sweaty skin. Sitting on the edge of the sofa, she hummed the only song she knew, "Lullaby and Goodnight."[1] Henry's eyes fluttered open, recognizing the song. It was the one his mother used to sing to him at bedtime. He managed a feeble smile. She dipped the cloth in the bowl of water, wrung it out, and laid it on his throat.

Mr. Dan walked in. "Miss Nellie, Miss Minnie wants you to go to the kitchen to help with dinner. I'll take over here."

"Okay." She patted Henry on the arm and stood. "Hope you feel better." Henry's eyes fluttered open for a moment, then closed again.

Mr. Dan got a bowl of fresh water and let the cloth soak up the cool liquid. He squeezed it out and gently patted Henry's face. Henry fell asleep to the sound of the ticking clock.

"Aarrgghh." Henry woke with a start. "Ooowww!" He writhed in pain.

"What's the matter, Henry?" Hoping off the sofa, Mr. Dan got on his knees and leaned over the sick boy.

"My stomach. It hurts!"

"Mr. Dan, I came as soon as I could. What's wrong?" Miss Fannie asked.

"Headache, sweating, nausea, and belly pain. I've got to go. Can you sit with him for a few minutes?"

"Yes, of course." She sat down and brushed the hair off his forehead. She glanced around the room, then whispered, "I heard what happened yesterday. I'm proud of you, Henry. You were brave to do what many of us have been unable or unwilling to do."

Henry blinked his eyes open and focused on her face. "Really?"

"Yes, really." Miss Fannie smiled.

"Oh! It hurts," Henry whimpered.

"Shh. You'll be okay, I promise." The dorm door slammed, startling Miss Fannie.

"Why wasn't Henry in class this morning or at dinner?" Miss Gertrude smirked at the sick boy with contempt.

1. Johannes Brahms, "Lullaby and Goodnight," 1868.

"He's very sick," Miss Fannie said.

"What's wrong with him?"

"He's got a headache, nausea, and abdominal pain. He's also been sweating."

"Do what you need to do. Make sure he's well enough to do his job this afternoon!" She left without another word.

Miss Fannie's shoulders drooped. "She wants him to do his job this afternoon." She shook her head.

At four o'clock Mr. Dan walked Henry to the barn. "Sit here. Eddy and me will take care of the animals."

"Yes, sir." Henry leaned against one of the stalls and hugged his knees.

When they were done, Mr. Dan took Henry to the dorm to wash up and change into fresh clothes. Henry nibbled at his food at suppertime. Mr. Dan took Henry back to the Anhorns' quarters until fifteen to nine, when he took him to his room.

"Sammy, I want you to keep an eye on Henry tonight. If he gets worse, come get me. Understand?"

"Yes, sir." Mr. Dan left and Sammy sat on the edge of Henry's cot. "How you feeling?"

"Bad."

"Then I guess you don't want to play cards?"

The corners of Henry's mouth curled up slightly. "Maybe tomorrow," Henry whispered.

....

Thursday, October 19, 1905

Henry yawned. After a night of restless sleep, he lay awake on his cot. Sammy sat up and stretched. "Was that the knock on the door?" Sammy asked.

"Yeah." Henry yawned again.

"How do you feel?"

"I'm tired, but my head doesn't hurt as bad, and I'm not sweating. My stomach feels a little better, too."

"Good. C'mon, let's go."

Miss Nellie placed a bowl of grits and a biscuit in front of Henry. "Hope you can eat this morning."

Henry's appetite had returned. "I think I can." He scooped up a spoonful of creamy grits and ate. Henry managed to eat half the grits and part of the biscuit. By midafternoon, Henry was vomiting. The stomach cramps had returned with a vengeance. At bedtime, the diarrhea set in.

22

Friday-Saturday, October 20-21, 1905

For the next two days, Henry lay on the sofa in the Anhorns' living quarters. His weakened body shivered with chills, and his temperature climbed. Muscle pain set in. Still vomiting, he was unable to eat. The only thing he could do was sip water. Miss Nellie, Miss Fannie, Mr. Dan, and Ruth took turns staying by Henry's side.

....

Sunday, October 22, 1905

Sunlight poured into the sitting room, illuminating the small, crumpled body on the sofa. There was a chill to the air, but Mr. Dan didn't notice as he crossed the distance from the barn to the dormitory. "I'm here, Miss Fannie."

"Morning, Dan." Exhausted, she stood. "I want you to look at his face and his eyes. Tell me what you see."

Mr. Dan kneeled down and took Henry's chin in his fingers. He turned Henry's face left and right, then pulled open his eyelids. "Hm. There's a yellow cast to his skin and eyes."

"That's what I was afraid of—he has jaundice. He's a very sick little boy. Thank God his parents are coming today. They can get him the care he needs."

Henry's eyes fluttered open. "What day is it?"

"It's Sunday. Your parents are coming today," Mr. Dan said. He brushed Henry's hair out of his eyes. "You know, if I had a son, I'd want him to be like you."

"You mean that?"

"I sure do." Mr. Dan's eyes crinkled.

....

The children waited on the porch for their parents to arrive. Miss Fannie walked out and saw Grace leaning against the building, twisting her hair. "Grace, how are you dear?" Grace stared at the teacher and said nothing. Miss Fannie's heart sank. *I've got to get her away from here!*

Ruth didn't know what to expect when her father and Kate got to Pinehurst. She knew her father would be upset that Henry was sick. She didn't realize just how upset he'd be or just how sick Henry truly was. She paced on the porch waiting for Hercules to make the turn up the drive. Ruth stepped off the porch and shaded her eyes from the bright sunlight. "Where are they?" She heard the gelding snorting before she saw him. Herman had barely got Hercules to a stop before Ruth reached for her father's arm.

"My goodness, Ruthie, a bit excited today?" Herman smiled. Looking at her expression, he knew something wasn't right. "What is it, Ruthie? What's wrong?" He jumped down and quickly scanned the area. "Where's Henry?"

"Oh, Father! Henry is sick. He's in the downstairs of the dormitory."

Miss Gertrude came out and got Herman's attention. "Hello, Mr. Conrader. I'm sorry to say Henry is not feeling well. Please come with me."

They quickly followed Miss Gertrude into the schoolhouse. Herman asked, "What's wrong with Henry?" They walked through the building at a fast clip and out the back door.

"He's had a headache and has been vomiting. Today he woke with a fever."

"My God, it sounds serious. Can we hurry, please?" She led them to the room with the sofa where Henry lay. Miss Gertrude opened the drapes all the way. Mr. Dan stood and stepped aside. Herman knelt down. "Henry, son, can you hear me?" Herman placed his hand on Henry's head. Turning to Kate, he said, "His fever is high."

Ruth stood back, chewing on her fingernails, watching and listening. Blinking, Henry tried to focus his glassy eyes on his father. "Father?" he whispered.

Startled with Henry's condition, Herman's back went stiff. He leaned back, then closer to Henry. He lifted his eyelids. "He's got jaundice! How long has he had it?" Herman's voice shook as it grew louder.

"Since early this morning," Miss Gertrude said.

"We've got to take him to a doctor! Now!"

"Mr. Conrader, I'm sure he will be fine. He just needs a couple of days to recuperate."

"I don't think so, Miss Gertrude!" Herman picked up Henry, dropping the quilt to the floor. "Kate, get his quilt!" Kate scooped it up and followed Herman toward the door.

Hearing the commotion, Sammy scooted down the stairs. "Henry's leaving?"

"Yes. He's very sick. He needs to go to a doctor," Ruth sniffed.

Herman cradled Henry in his arms and left the dormitory. Ruth opened the back door to the schoolhouse. Walking at a fast pace, Herman headed into the building. Kate and Miss Gertrude were close behind. "Really, Mr. Conrader, I think you're overreacting. Henry will be fine," Miss Gertrude called out.

Kate stopped and spun around to face Miss Gertrude. "Fine? You think he'll be fine?" Kate roared, her face reddening. She shook her finger in Miss Gertrude's face. "How dare you presume Henry's fine. You should've contacted a doctor and us days ago!" Kate's cold, hard eyes stared into the face of evil.

"Mrs. Conrader, I do not appreciate your attitude or behavior toward me."

"Oh, you don't, don't you? Listen here, Miss Gertrude. We entrusted you with the care of Henry and Ruth and you failed. You failed miserably. Now shut your mouth and leave us alone!"

As Herman passed the library, he called out, "Can I please get some help here?" Mr. Bingham rushed past them and opened the front door.

Ignoring what Kate had said, Miss Gertrude, now red in the face, called out, "Mr. Conrader! You can't take Henry and Ruth out just like that!"

Herman whipped around and stared her in the face with fury in his eyes. "You let my son get sick and stay sick for God knows how long! This is an emergency! Why didn't you take him to the doctor? Why didn't you notify us he was sick? He's got the advanced symptoms of yellow fever. I lived through the yellow jack epidemic of '88 and watched people I knew and loved die. I will not lose Henry, too! Now leave us alone!"

Mr. and Mrs. Hinsky, Will's parents, were taken aback at what they had witnessed. Mr. Bingham was stunned with Miss Gertrude's behavior. Alex's father shook his head. They stood around talking about what had just happened. The children were speechless.

"Mr. and Mrs. Hinsky, Mr. Johnsen, Mr. and Mrs. Bingham, please. Don't let this little episode upset you! Mr. Conrader is overreacting. Henry's fine."

Mr. Bingham cocked his head and looked at Miss Gertrude in disbelief. "Excuse me, Madam, Mr. Conrader was not overreacting; we all saw the boy. Our children told us he's been sick for almost a week. I find your flippant attitude and lack of concern disturbing. I cannot speak for the others, but Eddy and David will be leaving your 'model school' at the end of the month."

Mr. Hinsky spoke up, "Mr. Bingham, we're with you. Will is leaving as well, Miss Gertrude."

"But you can't! Your children are thriving here. You'd be making a big mistake. There's no other school around which can offer what Pinehurst does."

Mr. Johnsen turned to Alex. "Son, let's get you packed up. We're leaving."

"Please, don't be rash. We here at Pinehurst take pride in the work we do for the children. Many of our former students have gone on to colleges and universities."

"That's all well and good. However, it's too little too late. Alex, let's go," Mr. Johnsen said.

Fannie and Dan stood in the doorway and listened to Gertrude's tirade. "It was bound to happen, Dan. She cares more about this 'school' than she ever did for the children. As much as it will affect us all, I'm glad that some are able to leave. Unfortunately, it's not so easy for us."

"Yes, ma'am. I know what you mean. You know, I'm going to miss Henry. Such a good-hearted boy. Who would've thought it would be him that brought Miss Gertrude to her knees?"

Fannie smiled. "I'll miss him, too."

....

Jacksonville

"Whoa!" Herman pulled hard on the reins, stopping in front of 311 East First Street. "Ruth, call Doctor Duer. Kate, prepare his bed." He jumped down, went to the backseat, and pulled Henry toward him. "Everything will be all right, son." Herman choked back tears. He picked up the fragile boy and carried him through the front door and upstairs.

Ruth ran upstairs. "Doctor Duer said he'd be here right away." She stood in the doorway of Henry's room wiping away tears. "Will he get better, Father?"

"Yes, Ruthie. Go get a bowl of water and a cloth for me." Herman checked his watch: seven-thirty. Ruth brought in the water and handed her father the cloth. "Go downstairs and wait for the doctor."

Placing her hand on his shoulder, Kate said, "Herman, what can I do?"

"Pray. Pray to God he survives this." Tears streamed down Herman's face. He dampened the cloth and placed it on Henry's feverish brow.

Bam. Bam. Bam. Ruth flung the door open. "Doctor! It's Henry. He's really sick. He's in his room."

Jim Duer bounded up the stairs. "Herman, what are his symptoms?" He took his stethoscope from his bag and listened to Henry's chest.

"Chills, fever, vomiting, abdominal pain, and jaundice." Herman's voice quavered. "Jim, I'm so afraid it's yellow fever," Herman's voice was laden with worry.

"Let me take a look." Dr. Duer took Henry's temperature and checked his pulse. "Hm. Temperature is 102, and his pulse is weak and rapid." The doctor palpated Henry's belly. "Don't feel anything remarkable here." He quickly examined Henry's arms and legs. Lifting the boy's eyelids, he frowned. "Jaundice is apparent in the eyes and skin." Dr. Duer took Henry's arms and pulled them out straight.

"Ooowww!"

"He's got muscle pain as well. Herman, I want to admit him to St. Luke's Hospital and run some tests. It might be yellow fever, but I'm leaning more toward malaria. Help me take him to the car."

Herman rode in the back seat with Henry's head in his lap. "Please, dear God. I can't lose him," he whispered. Herman shook, weeping.

....

Henry lay in the hospital bed, floating in and out of a restless sleep. His glassed-over eyes gazed into space. "Where am I?" Henry whispered.

"You're in the hospital; the doctor says you'll be fine."

"Father?"

"Yes, Henry! I'm here. Shh. Don't try to talk. I'm with you now." Henry's eyes closed. Herman sat at Henry's side, holding his hand. The stress of the long day took its toll, and Herman drifted off. When he awoke, Dr. Duer was on the other side of the bed listening to Henry's chest.

"Herman, there's a ninety-five percent chance he's got malaria. There've been reports of large populations of the *Anopheles* mosquito in neighboring counties—the type which carries the malarial parasite. He must've been bitten by this type of mosquito."

"But he doesn't have any bites. How can that be?"

"It can take weeks for malaria to show up. Symptoms of yellow fever take only a few days to appear after being infected by a mosquito, and we'd be able to see the remnants of bites on him. Because of this, I feel confident in saying it's not yellow fever."

....

Monday, October 23, 1905

Herman stood and stretched. He walked to one of the windows and parted the drapes. The morning light streamed into the sterile white room. He pulled the drapes open and returned to Henry's bedside. Placing his hand on Henry's brow, he noticed Henry's fever had diminished. "Thank you, God," Herman whispered.

Kate opened the door to the children's ward and peeked her head into the room. Seeing Herman sitting by a bed in the corner of the room, she tiptoed over to him. "Herman, how is he?" she asked.

"Kate! He's doing better; low to no fever. I'm not sure, but the jaundice doesn't seem to be as bad as it was yesterday. Jim said he'd recover. He's got to stay here for a couple more days before he can come home, though."

"I'm so glad he'll be okay, Herman." Kate took Herman's hand and gave it a squeeze.

"Can you imagine what might've happened had we not gone for a visit yesterday? I shudder at the thought."

"I know," she whispered. A tear rolled down her cheek.

Henry's condition continued to improve. By Wednesday evening his jaundice and muscle pain had disappeared. Dr. Duer discharged him the following afternoon.

23

Friday, October 27, 1905

Henry awoke and stretched, glad to be in his own bed. Ruth popped her head in before leaving for school. "Are you feeling any better?"

"A little, I guess. I'm tired, though."

"Well, at least you don't have to worry about feeding animals after breakfast!"

"I know. I can't believe we're home. You know, it feels like it's been one big, bad nightmare. I'll miss Sammy and Jack. And Eddy, too. I guess I can write to them."

"You don't know, do you?"

"Don't know what?"

"Eddy's parents are pulling him and David out of Pinehurst at the end of the month. Will's and Alex's parents pulled them out last Sunday too."

"Really?"

"Yes, their parents were there when Father told Miss Gertrude we were leaving. They decided to take the boys out then."

"Wow. I wonder what will happen to the rest of the kids."

"I don't know. I need to leave now—I'll see you after school," Ruth said.

"Okay, bye." Henry yawned again. He went to the bathroom to wash his face. Feeling a bit woozy, Henry returned to his bed.

"Good morning, Henry. How are you?" Kate smiled. She set a tray with his breakfast on his dresser.

"Okay, but I got a little dizzy."

"I imagine it will still take a few days for you to feel like your old self."

The rich smell of buttered oatmeal and biscuits with gravy drifted to his nose, making his stomach growl. "I'm hungry!"

"Good. You need to build your strength," Kate said, placing the tray in front of Henry. "I'm glad you're home." Kate sat on the end of the bed while Henry ate.

"Me, too." Henry smiled.

That afternoon Henry heard the front door open, then close with a thud. A moment later Ruth poked her head into Henry's room. "Hi, Henry."

"Guess what?"

"I don't know, what?" Ruth sat on the edge of his bed.

"I got a letter today from Miss Fannie! Let me read it to you."

Dear Henry,

I hope you are doing well. Things aren't the same here without you. Mr. Dan says the cows and horses miss you, and they wish you'd come back. It's unfortunate Buster and Bella could not be with you and Ruth at home. Sammy is taking care of them now.

Sammy and Jack are doing well, although it's now just the two of them cleaning stalls. I'll let you in on a little secret—Sammy is leaving Pinehurst at the end of the term in December. His parents heard what happened to you and they are sending him to his old school beginning in January. But the best part? Sammy's parents are adopting Jack! He will finally have a loving family to call his own.

Another student has left the school. Grace went back to the orphanage yesterday. Although it's not the best situation, I think it's better for her than Pinehurst. Hopefully she will find a family soon.

I know you left in a rush and were unable to take your belongings. I know how much your mother meant to you, so I wanted to return her photograph to you.

I wish you well in all you do.

Sincerely,

Miss Fannie

Henry held up the photograph. "I'm so happy Miss Fannie mailed Mother's picture back to me! So the animals miss me!" Henry laughed. "I'm happy Jack will finally have a family." Henry's smile disappeared. "I wish we could've brought the dogs home with us. I miss Buster."

"I miss Bella, too." Ruth pressed her lips together. They sat in silent contemplation.

Finally, Henry spoke. "I don't know, Ruth. What do you think? Should we tell them what went on there?"

"I'm not sure. Part of me wants to, but then part of me says no. I don't know what good it would do."

"Me either, but I think they'd want to know." Henry gazed out the window, his thoughts drifting to the first time he was punished at Pinehurst.

....

After supper Herman and Kate retired to the parlor. "It sure is good to have them home," Herman said.

"Yes, it is." Kate placed her hand on Herman's.

"Is it me, or is Henry acting different to you?" Herman asked.

"I think he's changed a little. Perhaps a bit more mature?"

"Could be."

Ruth and Henry stood in the doorway of the parlor. Ruth tapped on the wall. "Father, Kate, may we talk to you?" she asked, barely audible. Henry stepped from behind his sister and peered at his father.

"Yes, of course! What is it?" Herman's eyebrows drew close together.

"It's about Pinehurst. Things happened there. We thought we should tell you." Henry said.

"What kind of things?" Herman's eyes stayed on Henry.

"We all had jobs. And not only the job in the garden. Hard jobs. Mine was feeding and watering the cows and horses twice a day, every day." Henry bowed his head.

"My job was housekeeping." Ruth listed off her duties.

Herman gaped. "Why didn't you tell me this before?"

"We weren't allowed to. We were told we'd be punished if we told our parents about the jobs and the, the . . ."

"The what, Ruth, what?"

"The horrible punishment," Henry whispered.

"What kind of punishment?" Perspiration dampened Herman's brow.

"If somebody broke a rule, they would be hit on their bottoms with a leather strap a few times. If they did something bad, they'd be put in a tiny closet, too. Sometimes for hours," Ruth said.

"Good God! Were you two punished?"

Ruth shook her head no. She looked at Henry and squeezed her eyes shut, a tear dripping from her chin. "Yes, sir," Henry said, letting out a quiet moan. Henry recounted each time he broke a rule and the type of punishment he received. "I, I tried to tell you. I wrote a letter to you. Miss Gertrude didn't mail it; she kept it and read it. I got in a lot of trouble."

Herman sat motionless, looking at Henry with a pained stare. He opened his mouth to speak, then closed it. His face reddened and his nostrils flared. "How could she? I can understand the need for discipline at the school, but to beat children? And put them in a closet for hours?" Herman's voice shook. "I'm contacting the authorities to see what they can do about this!"

....

Henry went to his room and crawled into bed. *I'm so glad to be home. I can't believe how much I missed Father and Kate.* A warm feeling stirred inside him. Kate tapped on the door and asked if she could come in.

"Yes, I'm still awake," Henry said.

Kate sat on the edge of his bed rubbing her hands together. "Henry, I have something I want to say to you."

Feelings of uneasiness fluttered through him. "Okay."

A tear trickled down her cheek. "I'm sorry. I'm sorry for sending you to Pinehurst. It was a bad decision, and I regret it. I'm sorry for all the horrible things you went through."

Henry remained silent for a moment, letting her apology sink in. "It's okay. It's not your fault Miss Gertrude is so mean. You didn't know."

"I hope you can find it in your heart to forgive me."

Henry got up and sat beside her. "I do forgive you." He put his arms around Kate and they sat together in silence holding each other.

....

Saturday, October 28, 1905

Knock. Knock. Knock. Henry heard the front door open. A minute later, Kate tapped on Henry's door as she opened it. "Henry, you have a visitor." She stepped aside and let Thomas into the bedroom.

"Thomas!"

"Hi, Henry. I heard you were home, and you've been sick. You doing okay now?"

"Yeah, I feel better. I had malaria. I was sick for a couple of weeks."

"I'm glad you're home. I've missed my best friend."

"So what've you been doing?"

"Nothing, really. Just going to school. I wish you were there."

"I will be—I'm not going back to Pinehurst. I'm staying here!"

"Really? That's great, Henry! When do you start back?"

"Probably Monday. It'll be strange. It's so different from Pinehurst."

"Yeah? So what was it like?" Thomas asked. Henry remained silent. "Henry?"

"It was a nightmare." Henry started at the beginning, telling him about the suspicions he had when they pulled up in front of the school for the first time. "I don't know what it was, but I had this feeling that something was bad, almost evil, about this place. I was right." His eyes glazed over. His monotone voice continued, telling Thomas about the work they were assigned to do, and the punishment Miss Gertrude handed out so freely.

"I can't believe she put you in a tiny closet."

"That was the worst part. Worse than getting whipped. Then one day something in me changed. I told Miss Gertrude I knew it was her that unlatched a stall door so I would be blamed for it. She got furious and punished me twice as much."

"You told her that? Wow!"

"Yeah." Henry shook his head as if to fling the depressing thoughts out of it.

"Did you ever get to have any fun?"

"Yeah." Henry's lip curled up. He told Thomas about the times he and the others snuck out at night, and the animals they saw. "I had a dog, too, and I named him Buster. My roommate there taught me a couple of card games. I'll teach them to you."

"Okay." Thomas glanced at Henry's clock. "I've got to go now."

Henry frowned at the thought of Thomas leaving. "Can you come over tomorrow afternoon?"

"I'll ask. Maybe we can go to the river if you feel up to it."

"Yeah, okay," Henry said.

24

Saturday, November 4, 1905

"You sure you're okay with this?" Herman dried the plate and placed it in the cabinet.

"Yes, it's fine, really," Kate smiled. "I think it will do them both a world of good." She put the dishcloth down and put her arms around him. "It's a wonderful idea."

"It's perfect timing, too. Mrs. Friganza came into the store yesterday and told me they'd be ready today. How about we walk over after dinner?"

"Splendid! I'm so excited for them—I can't wait to see their faces!"

Herman called for Henry and Ruth to come downstairs. "Mrs. Friganza has asked us to come over this afternoon. I'd like to leave in a few minutes."

"Okay, Father," Ruth said.

"Aw. Do I have to go?" Henry asked.

"Yes, we're all going. We won't stay long. Go upstairs and wash up."

"Yes, sir." Henry took his time ascending the stairs.

....

The family walked the three blocks to East Fourth Street and took a left on Walnut. They arrived at the Friganzas' home, a light-blue Queen Anne-style house trimmed in white. Henry raced up the steps of the porch and tapped the door knocker. A moment later, Maggie Friganza opened the door and greeted the visitors. "Hello. Won't you please come in." Buffy, the Friganza's beagle, trotted up behind her.

"Oh, how cute!" Ruth dropped to her knees. Henry joined in, showering the dog with affection. Buffy's tail wagged—she was enjoying the attention. Herman turned to Kate and winked.

Mrs. Friganza smiled. "Come with me."

They followed her to the enclosed back porch. She opened the door and eight beagle puppies scampered toward them. *Yip! Yip! Yip!* "Oh, my goodness!" Ruth beamed.

"There's so many of them!" Henry laughed and plopped down on the floor, letting the puppies climb on his lap. Ruth took a seat beside him and picked one up, placing it in her lap. Henry and Ruth played with the puppies while the adults spoke in whispers.

"Are any of them taken yet?" Herman asked.

"No, they can choose whichever ones they want," Mrs. Friganza said.

"Fantastic. Kate, do you want to tell them?"

Kate smiled and nodded. "Henry, Ruth, it's almost time to go." Both Henry's and Ruth's expressions soured, their smiles disappearing. "But before we leave, make sure you pick out your new puppy."

"What! Really?" Henry jumped up.

"We can get one? Wow!" Ruth's eyes opened wide.

"You can each pick one!" Kate said, smiling and clapping.

Henry and Ruth looked at each other and grinned. "Yippee!" Henry bounced on his toes. "I can't believe it!" He scanned the room and was overwhelmed by the choices. "I don't know which one to choose!" Henry sat and once again the puppies paraded across his lap, stumbling. He glanced around, surveying the litter, when he noticed a lone puppy under a chair.

"Oh!" Henry went over to it and carefully pulled the puppy out. It licked his hand. Henry smiled. He ran his hand across its back. The puppy responded by wagging its tail. It licked him again. "He's so friendly!"

Mrs. Friganza giggled. "Henry, he is a she. She's a little girl."

"A girl! Well, I guess it's okay." A grin stretched across his face.

"I found one!" Ruth picked her up and touched her nose to the puppy's nose.

Herman said, "You two ready to take them home?"

"Yes!" Ruth said.

"Yes, sir!" Henry hugged the puppy. "I think I'll call her Ginger! Ruth, what are you going to name yours?"

"Hmmm. I like 'Princess.'" She held the puppy up to her face. "Hi, Princess!" The puppy licked Ruth's nose. "I think she likes her name!" They got the dogs ready to go and headed for the front door. The children thanked Mrs. Friganza for the puppies and promised to take good care of them.

....

Friday, November 17, 1905

Thump. Kate looked at the time: six o'clock. "Herman, is that you?" Kate walked out of the kitchen, drying her hands with a dishtowel.

"Yes, dear." Herman placed his hat and coat on the rack and ran his hand through his hair. He went to the parlor and took a seat. He rubbed his eyes.

"What's wrong?"

"I went to the courthouse today and talked to Judge McLean."

"And?" Taking his hand, Kate sat next to Herman.

"He told me nothing can be done about what happened at Pinehurst. Since corporal punishment is legal, Miss Gertrude didn't break any laws. He also said it would be Henry's word against hers in civil court, and the chances of winning a suit are slim, at best." Leaning back in his chair, Herman's shoulders slumped.

"Herman, I'm sorry. I know you wanted to make Miss Gertrude pay for what she did to the children." Blinking away tears, she gave her husband's hand a gentle squeeze.

"I have to turn this over to a higher authority. I've got to believe Miss Gertrude will be held responsible on her day of reckoning," Herman said, his voice thick. They sat together in silence, the clock ticking away the minutes.

....

Saturday, November 25, 1905

"Henry!" Kate yelled. Looking out the kitchen window, she watched Ginger go under the shed. "Come down here, now!"

Henry's stomach rolled. He bolted down the stairs and into the kitchen. "Yes, ma'am?"

"It's Ginger—she's under the shed and has one of your father's socks! Run out there and try to get her to come out."

Henry ran outside to the shed and wriggled his way under it as far as he could go. "Ginger! Come here, girl." The puppy sat inches from Henry with the sock hanging out of her mouth. Henry made kissy sounds to encourage her to come closer. She didn't move. "Come on, Ginger."

Kate went back to the house and returned with a piece of cheese. "Here, try giving her this." Henry tempted the puppy. With one whiff of the cheese, Ginger dropped the sock and crawled out. Henry stood, picked her up, and handed her to Kate. He dropped back down to his stomach and crawled in to get the sock. Barely able to reach it, he grabbed it and backed out from under the small building.

Henry held the sock up. "Got it!" He smiled, then looked at it more closely. "Oh, no! It's full of holes!" Henry glanced at Kate with apprehension.

Kate pursed her lips. A moment later a smile crossed her face and she began to giggle. Her giggle turned into a laugh, and Henry joined in. "I suppose your father can wear his 'holy' socks to church!" They laughed until their sides hurt. "Come on, Henry. Let's go inside." Handing Ginger to him, she wiped the tears of laughter from her eyes. She put her arm around Henry as they walked back to the kitchen. "I don't remember the last time I laughed so much!"

"Yeah, me, too," Henry said, still giggling. He sat down at the kitchen table. Ginger licked his hand as he petted her. "Since Ginger is my responsibility, I want to buy Father another pair of socks."

"You do? That's considerate of you, Henry."

"Do you have any chores I can do to earn some money to buy them?"

"Well, I didn't get to the sweeping today in the parlor and the dining room. Would you like to do that?"

"Yes, ma'am." Henry put Ginger down and went to the closet to get the broom and dustpan.

. . .